Witch S

Book

Miss Moffat's Academy
for
Refined Young Witches

Katrina Kahler

clothes; her clothes. She could see two long antennae wriggling out in front of her and she took a step backwards to get away from them. The antennae moved with her and her legs, she no longer just had two, instead she had six.

Charlotte wasn't human any more, instead she had been turned into a cockroach. She crawled out from under the clothes and looked up at the giant smirking Margaret.

'My mom says that roaches are the worst kind of vermin so it seemed kinda fitting for you. See ya around, that's if you manage not to get squashed first,' she sniggered as she peered down at her.

Charlotte watched as Margaret strutted out of the room, she was left there wondering what to do now. Her teacher at her old school had told her once how cockroaches had been around for millions of years and that they could survive nuclear explosions. She hoped that this was true, as she didn't want to end up a crumpled mess on the bottom of someone's shoe. She worried if this spell would last forever unless she somehow managed to explain what'd happened to someone and get them to change her back.

Charlotte scurried across the room and flew up onto her bed. Her wings were weak but she managed to get them to work a bit.

She wondered if Margaret had been let back into the Academy or if she'd just snuck in to get revenge? Charlotte hoped that she wasn't back as she didn't want to look at her smug face every lesson if she managed to survive this.

The door swung open and Stef, Gerty and Alice entered the room and walked over to their beds.

4

'I wonder where Charlotte is?' Gerty asked, as she dropped down onto her bed.

'Dunno, hope she's not in any more trouble,' Stef replied.

'I don't see why she would be, she's not one for rule breaking.'

'True, although I hope she's not in any more trouble over the Margaret thing.'

'I hope not,' Gerty gave a worried look.

'I wonder where Margaret is?' Alice asked.

'I hope she's at the bad witches' school with no friends and rat soup for her lunch,' Stef said.

'Ew,' Gerty chuckled.

'If they try to serve us rat soup here my parents will be hearing about it,' Alice stuck her nose in the air.

Charlotte knew that she needed to get their attention...so she fluttered her flimsy wings and managed to find enough power to fly over to Gerty. She landed on her arm and tried getting her attention.

'Gerty, Gerty, it's me Charlotte,' she crawled up her arm.

Gerty looked down and saw the bug on her arm, she let out a shriek and tried swatting it away as she jumped up onto her feet.

'What is it?' Stef rushed over to her.

'C-c-cockroach,' she frantically flicked out her arm even though Charlotte had now fallen onto the floor.

Alice squealed and jumped up onto her bed, swiping away at the air.

'I'll find it,' Stef said, as she stomped her feet on the ground.

Charlotte darted out of the way and scurried under Alice's bed, which made her scream even louder.

'This is an outrage, wait until my parents hear about this,' Alice shrieked.

'Please, it's me,' Charlotte pleaded but no one could hear her words.

Stef continued to stomp her feet across the floor and Charlotte raced past her and managed to fly over to the open window and throw herself out of it. She half-flew, half-fell down and landed in a bush outside.

She wanted to cry, only she didn't think that cockroaches could. Her own friends had been terrified of her and had tried to squash her and now she was outside somewhere in the surroundings of the Academy not knowing what to do next.

She decided to keep on scurrying forwards, eventually she found herself in the flying area where a group of older students were being instructed by Miss Firmfeather as they whizzed around the arena.

A girl with long black hair landed her broomstick and Charlotte immediately began to climb it.

'Please, I'm a student here. I need help,' she said; only her voice came out as a buzzing sound.

'Yuck,' the girl said, as she flicked Charlotte off her broom and onto the ground.

'Please, I'm not a real cockroach,' Charlotte pleaded, as she scurried up another broomstick.

The broomstick began to shake and Charlotte tumbled onto the ground. Soon broomsticks were smashing against the ground and multiple feet were trying to stand on her. She weaved in-between them all before she hurried away.

She stayed out of sight and watched as the lesson finished and the girls left the flying arena.

Suddenly she smelt something and her antennae frantically moved in front of her. Before she could stop herself she was letting them lead her, until she found herself by the black trashcans at the back of the Academy.

One of the bins had been knocked over and garbage had spilled out onto the ground. She didn't want to go near it...yet she found herself with an overpowering craving to find food within the dirty, putrid trash.

She crawled over to it and rooted through it until she found a mouldy old sandwich. Before she could stop herself she was nibbling at it, enjoying the vulgar taste.

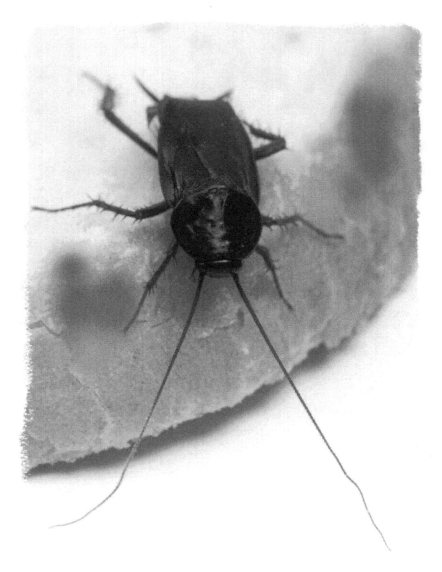

The next thing she knew the trash rose into the air and dropped into the now upright trash can, only Charlotte was still on the ground, and she wasn't a cockroach any more, instead she was back to being human. A piece of the mouldy sandwich was still in her mouth and she spat it out, a nauseous feeling rising inside of her as she wiped her mouth onto the back of her arm.

'What are you doing in the garbage?' a woman in a black apron said, as she stared at Charlotte. Her arms folded and a frown creased on her forehead.

Charlotte quickly wrapped her arms around her legs, aware that she had no clothes on. Her cheeks flushed redder than the beetroot her mom used in soup and she could still taste the mouldy sandwich on her lips.

'Wait here,' the woman said, she disappeared through a door and returned with an oversized jumper and a pair of baggy white trousers. 'The best I can do,' she threw then over at Charlotte.

'Thanks,' she replied, as she hurriedly got dressed.

She knew that she looked ridiculous as the trousers were at least two sizes too big on her and she had to hold them at the side so that they didn't fall down. However she definitely favored these clothes over no clothes at all and was grateful to the woman for helping her.

'You're not coming through my kitchen. You're filthy. You're have to walk the long way round,' the woman said, before she turned her back on Charlotte and walked off.

'Okay,' Charlotte nodded.

She turned her head and gave a piece of advice, 'I advise you to keep a wide berth from whoever decided to turn you into a cockroach.'
'I plan to,' Charlotte muttered.

Luckily classes were taking place so Charlotte managed to walk through the castle without being seen, at least that was until she got to the corridor that led to her room.

'Charlotte Smyth, why are you wearing that and why do you have bits of old food all over your face?'

Charlotte turned to face a very unimpressed looking Molly, her blonde hair tied into two pigtails that flowed down the front of her fitted school blouse.

'Erm I, erm it was. I'm sorry, it won't happen again,' she spluttered out, not wanting to mention Margaret in fear of more revenge attacks.

Margaret hadn't hesitated in turning her into a cockroach, so she dreaded to think what spell she'd cast on her next time. Charlotte felt as though she would never be able to compete with Margaret when it came to spells because Margaret had experience with spells whereas she didn't.

'We have standards at this school, don't let me see you like this again.'

Charlotte nodded, before she hurried over to her bedroom. She jumped into the shower but failed to fully get rid of the smell of garbage, as if it had embedded itself in her nose.

She changed into her uniform and used her wand to cast the hair-drying spell that Gerty had taught her. Afterwards she left her room to go and find the others, luckily it was currently a study lesson and she knew that they'd be in the library. She knew that the Mistress of the Books would probably give her a stern look, but as long as she didn't talk she shouldn't be in too much trouble.

She was not going to be defeated by Margaret Montgomery, even if that meant she had to spend the rest of her morning searching the library for anti-cockroach spells.

Charlotte knew that she belonged at this school and she wasn't going to let Margaret sabotage this.

Chapter Two

It was lunchtime and Charlotte was staring into her bowl of yellowy-colored soup that the bats had just placed in front of them all. Seeing food brought back memories of the mouldy sandwich and she had to force herself not to heave.

'Are you okay Charlotte, you look pale?' Gerty asked, as she grabbed a slice from the enormous baguette that spanned the entire length of the table.

'Yeah, fine,' she swallowed, as she brought her hand up to her mouth

'Where were you all morning? You're lucky that the Mistress of the Books only gave you a filthy look when you you eventually arrived,' Stef said.

'I don't really want to talk about it.'

'You're not in trouble again are you?' Gerty asked.

'I hope not,' Alice said, before she dipped a piece of bread in her soup. 'I can't be seen sharing a room with a troublemaker, it looks bad on my character.'

Stef tore a piece off her bread and chucked it at Alice, hitting her in the face. She gave Stef an annoyed look, before she went back to sipping her soup.

I had an unpleasant distraction,' she mumbled.

'Are you going to explain to us what you mean or are we supposed to guess? Stef asked.

'I think that we need some sort of code in future, so that if one of us gets turned into something we can alert each other.'

'Okay, you're going to have to explain what you're on about because now I'm confused,' Stef said.

'It's just been one of those mornings,' Charlotte pushed her barely touched bowl of soup away.

'Are you not eating that?' Stef asked, as she stared at Charlotte's bowl.

Charlotte shook her head, so Stef grabbed the bowl and transferred her spoon into it.

'Say if one of us got turned into a rat against our will, how could we signal this to the rest of us?'

'Squeak three times,' Gerty giggled.

'Bite Stef on the ankle,' Alice said, which caused Stef to glare at her.

'What if we couldn't squeak or bite? What if we were a slug or a snail?' Charlotte enquired.

'Leave a slime trail saying help,' Stef chuckled.

I was thinking more like we mark a spot on the floor in our room with chalk and then we can use our wands on any creature that stays put on it.'

'Has something happened?' Gerty looked at Charlotte.

'I was just thinking about the time Alice was turned into a

mouse, that's all,' she lied.

Charlotte thought about telling them about what had happened with Margaret but she didn't want them to feel sorry for her or think that she was a weak witch. She just hoped that they'd remember what the mark she was going to chalk in their bedroom would be for and that none of them would ever have to use it.

***

'So girls,' Miss Maker said, as she twirled a strand of her purple tinged dark hair around her finger. 'What potion would you like to make today?'

'Really, we get to choose?' Gerty asked.

'Yes, we will make the most popular suggestion.'

There were excited murmurs between the girls at the prospect of this but Miss Maker looked unfazed as she awaited their suggestions.
'How about a potion that makes us super-fast, then we'd be amazing at our next fitness lesson?' Gerty said.

'Miss Dread would not appreciate that being used during her lessons,' Alice said.

'No, I don't suppose she would,' Miss Maker chuckled.

Charlotte wanted to suggest that they make a potion to prevent spells from being cast upon them but she couldn't get the words out.

'An extra-time potion, so that we don't have to get up so early?' Stef suggested.

'That's stupid, I want one that makes all my clothes fold themselves,' Alice said.

'Boring,' Stef rolled her eyes. 'Besides, there's bound to be a spell for that.'

'How about a potion to talk to animals?' Gerty asked.

'Too complicated,' Miss Maker said.

'A potion to change our hair color,' Patricia said, as she flicked out a strand of her red hair.

'I don't want to change my hair color,' Demi sneered. 'I

wouldn't mind a beauty potion to make me look my best for the ball. It's only two weeks away and I want to look as gorgeous as possible.'

'That's a marvellous idea Demi,' Miss Maker smiled, as she readjusted her witch's hat slightly so that it remained somewhat wonky.
She turned around and began to pull items out of the labelled compartments that lined the wall behind her.

The ball would be the first time that they met the boys that attended the nearby wizard's school and they all wanted to look their best for it.

'I was going to suggest making a beauty potion but Demi beat me too it,' Stef huffed.

'It doesn't matter,' Charlotte smiled, trying to appease Stef.

'I hope it works,' Gerty said excitedly. 'I want to look older and for my hair to be extra shiny and to be taller. I'm fed-up with looking like I'm the youngest.'

'But you are the youngest,' Alice said.

'That doesn't mean I want to look like I am.'

Miss Maker caused a large pile of ingredients to float in front of her before she made sections from each separate with her wand. They floated over to each girl and landed on the board in front of their mini cauldrons.

'Right girls, make sure to listen carefully to this carefully or else the results could be catastrophic,' she looked over at their worried faces. 'Now, let's get started,' she winked.

'Firstly you will need a sprig of lavender,' she held up her sprig, before she placed it into her cauldron.

The rest of the girls carefully placed their lavender into their cauldron and eagerly awaited their next instructions. Charlotte tried to remain focused on Miss Maker, as she didn't want to become distracted and mess up her potion. 'Next you'll need a pinch of chestnut powder,' she picked up a small amount of the beige looking dust.

'How can we be sure we've measured it right?' Stef asked.

'If it fits between your thumb and forefinger then you should be fine.'

Stef picked up the chestnut powder three times before she settled on an amount and sprinkled it into her cauldron.

'Now take one cherry,' she picked it up by the stem. 'And throw it all in.'

Miss Maker hummed quietly to herself and waited until all the girls had finished.

'Now, take your essence of peppermint,' she lifted up a small bottle. 'And apply two teaspoons,' she poured it onto the spoon before she brought it up to her nose. 'Peppermint is such a delightful smell, it reminds me of the mints my grandmother makes at Christmas.'

'Now, I see you're all ready so let's continue,' she looked around the room. 'Now, stir once clockwise. Once anti-clockwise and then twice more clockwise Now, pick up your blossom tree petal,' she lifted a pinkish-white petal. 'And crumple it under your fingers and then sprinkle it in.'

'I hope I'm doing this right?' Gerty whispered to Charlotte. She smiled but didn't reply, as she was concentrating.

'Now stir your potion three times anti-clockwise and you're done,' she took her spoon out of her potion. 'Demi, you only stirred twice.'

'No, I'm sure I stirred three times.'

'I can assure you that it was only twice,' Stef gave a sly smile.

Demi shrugged before she stirred her potion one more time anti-clockwise.

'Looks like you're all done, now all that's left to do is to wait for the potions to settle and then sip it down.'

'How does this potion work?' Stef asked, as she peered down at her smoking cauldron.

'I can't know for sure, as potions vary.'

'It will be good results though won't it?' Alice asked.

Miss Maker smiled, 'Of course, why do you think all your teachers look so young and beautiful? I think that your potions would have settled by now, so go ahead.'

Demi was the first girl to pour the potion into her glass but she waited until she saw that other girls had drunk theirs before she took a sip from it. Gerty and Charlotte exchanged looks before they both emptied their glasses.

'Do I look any different?' Stef said, her arm on her waist.

'No,' Charlotte shook her head.

'This potion doesn't work,' Demi sighed.

'I suggest that you give it time to bloom,' the teacher chuckled.

The girls glanced around at each other as they tried to spot signs that the spell was working. They were beginning to think that the spell was a dud and that nothing would happen, that was until Stef gave Gerty a double-look.

'Gerty, you look different,' Stef said, as she stared at her. 'You look younger.'

'Younger! How can I look younger?' she looked horrified, as she touched her face.

'You look slightly shorter too,' Alice chimed in.

'No I don't,' Gerty fought back tears.

'You look fine Gerty,' Charlotte said, as she looked down at her arms, noticing how her cardigan had become baggier on her.

'They've gone, where did they go?' Demi shouted, as she looked down at her chest. 'I want them back right now.'

Stef began to laugh as she looked over at Demi's hysterics. Demi was the only girl in their class who needed a bra and this potion had made her as flat chested as the rest of them.

You're as flat as an iron,' Stef snorted.

'Shush,' Charlotte said to Stef, followed by a wink.

'Miss Maker, this spell was supposed to make us look good, yet we all look like little kids. You must reverse the spell immediately!' Demi insisted.

'Nonsense, you all look beautiful,' Miss Maker smiled.

'I look stupid, I need to be back to normal,' Demi grasped her arms across her chest.

'You'll have to wait until the spell wears off.'

'What! But the ball is next week,' Stef said.

'You'll be back to normal in a few weeks.'

On hearing this, the room was filled with groans and disgruntled looks from the girls.

'Are you saying that we could be stuck looking like this at the ball?' Demi said.

'It's hard to know with magic. None of you need to worry, you all look glowing.'

'I don't want to look glowing, I want to look my age,' Demi growled.

'That's it for today, now clear up your cauldrons and then you can go,' Miss Maker addressed the girls. Begrudgingly the girls did as Miss Maker said, including Demi, although she took the longest to tidy up as she refused to move one of her arms away from her chest. Once they'd all tidied up Miss Maker dismissed them and they headed for the door.

'Bye girls,' Miss Maker said cheerily.

'Bye,' Charlotte said, forcing a smile. She was annoyed at the effects of the potion, but Miss Maker was still her favorite teacher and she didn't want to appear anything but polite towards her.

'This sucks,' Stef said, when they were out of earshot of Miss Maker.

it's not fair!
We look like 8 year olds!!!

'It's not so bad,' Gerty jumped on the spot. 'I have some lip-gloss and baby pink eyeshadow we can use at the ball.'

'Great,' Stef rolled her eyes. 'Not only will I look like a little kid, I will also look like Barbie doll.'

'Stef,' Charlotte glared at her.

'Sorry Gerty,' Stef sighed. 'I just really wanted to look good for the ball.'

'You always look good,' Gerty smiled.

'All that matters is that we're all be together at the ball, forget the boys,' Charlotte said.

'You're right, I can't wait,' Gerty squealed.

'My mother has a room full of make-up at home, I'd ask her to send some of it over to me, but it's very expensive,' Alice said.

'It doesn't matter Alice, I'm sure Gerty's lip-gloss will be just fine,' Charlotte smiled.

'Who needs boys anyway? Stef said.

'Yeah, they like dirt and find stupid jokes funny,' Gerty said.

'Yeah, we don't need them,' Stef put her arms around Gerty and Charlotte's shoulders. 'Girl's rule and boys drool.'

'Ew,' laughed Gerty.

'You could try asking your mom about the make-up Alice, if you tell her that you look about eight she might take pity on you,' Stef grinned.

'I do not look eight,' she gave an indignant look.

'Just messing,' chuckled Stef.

'Not funny,' Alice smiled.

They all continued up the corridor, the thought of the ball and the prospect of meeting the boys from the Wizard's School at the forefront of their minds.

Chapter Three

For the last week the main topic echoing through the corridors was about the school ball. The new students were talking about what refreshments would be served, what songs would be played and most importantly what the boys from the Wizard's School would be like. Whilst the older girls were discussing the boys by name, what outfit they'd be wearing and any potions that could improve their image, dancing and what they should say to boys. The Academy was at one with excitement and the mood was electric.

It was only an hour until they left for the Wizard's College and Charlotte and the others were getting ready.

'Whose taken my sparkly red ballet pumps?' Alice said, as she looked from girl-to-girl accusingly.

'I haven't seen them,' Gerty replied.

'My aunt brought them for me from a boutique in Paris and they aren't where I left them.'

'Nope, not seen them,' Stef shrugged, as she held up two dresses. 'Blue or green?'

'I like the blue one,' Charlotte said.

'Yeah, me too,' Gerty said.

'Both would clash terribly with my shoes, so give them back.'

'I don't have your stupid shoes,' Stef groaned, as she put the green dress down on her bed and hung onto the blue one.

There was a knock at the door and all the girls turned to look at it.

'Come in,' Gerty said.

The door opened and in walked Sonya and Silvia, both of them looking stunning in strappy knee-length dresses, Sonya's in baby blue and Silvia's in magenta.

'Who put this there,' Sonya said, as she tripped over a red shoe that was by the door, managing to grab onto the doorframe to steady her balance.

'Erm, that's mine,' Alice rushed over and picked up the shoe, a sheepish look on her face.

'You both look great,' Charlotte said.

'Thanks,' they replied in unison.

'You both look beautiful and I still look like a little kid,' Gerty bounced down onto her bed.

'No you don't Gerty, you look good,' Sonya said, as she took in Gerty's pretty pink floral dress.

'You know the potion has worn off, thank goodness,' Stef said, as she tied the sash on her dress.

'I know but I still look younger than the rest of you.'

'Well you are younger,' Stef said.

'You look great,' Charlotte smiled. 'And I love your dress.'

'It's cute isn't it?'

'Very.'

'We're just checking by from room to room to see how everyone's getting on?' Sonya said.

'We're nearly done,' Stef said.

'What are the boys like?' Gerty asked.

'The same as any other boys really. Some are cute, some make your skin cruel,' Silvia said.

'Do you remember that boy from the last ball, the one with the manically crazy hair that wouldn't stop following you around?' Sonya looked at her sister.

'Don't remind me,' she shook her shoulders. 'I had to hide under the refreshment table at one point just to get away from him.'

'Will there be boys from established wizard families there as I can't be seen dancing with just anyone,' Alice said, as she patted down the material of her cream dress.

'What makes you think they'd want to dance with you anyway?' Stef said.

'Alice, I have no idea. You'll just have to ask them when you're there,' said Sonya.

'I shouldn't have to ask them anything, a boy from an established family should come over to me and begin the conversation.'

'I don't think they'll be walking around with neon lights on them saying where they're from, not unless you try a spell,' Stef chuckled.

'Alice, we suggest you go to the ball intent on having a good time and if you find a boy, established or not, then so be it,' Sonya said.

'What boy could resist those shoes,' Gerty pointed down at Alice's feet, she'd found the other shoe under her bed and now had both of them on.

'They are Dorothy shoes, I like them when I'm not tripping over them,' Sonya said.

'My grandmother got them for me from Paris, from a very expensive shop,' Alice moved to the side to show them off better.

'We had better go check on the other girls. When you're ready head down to the great hall, Molly will be waiting there for you,' Silvia gave a wave as she headed out of the door, her sister following her.

'Let's go,' said Stef, as she grabbed her wand off her bed and threaded it through the sash on her dress.

'Are you sure I look okay?' Gerty said, as she did a spin that caused her dress to flow out like an upside-down umbrella.

'You look great, now let's go and dance,' Charlotte grabbed Gerty's arm and led her over to the door.

'Come on Dorothy,' Stef looked back over at Alice who was

rummaging through the pile of clothes on her bed. 'You can't be late for the Emerald City.'

Alice grabbed her wand off her bed and hurried over to the others.

***

Molly was stood in front of the staff table on the platform in the grand hall. She was wearing a corseted black-netted dress and she wore a black heart shaped clip in the side of her hair.

'Right everyone, a few rules before we head off to the wizard's college. No spiking the punch bowl with magic, no using love spells on the boys and remember that you are representing the Academy, therefore you must be on your best behavior at all times.

Right, follow me in an orderly fashion outside,' she walked down off the stage and then gestured for them to follow her out of the side door.

'I'm so excited,' Gerty said to Charlotte, as they followed the crowd of students towards the door.

'Me too,' replied Charlotte, as she managed to move her foot just in time before a girl in high heels stood on it.

They squashed through the doorway and out into the yard where a circular gold and black carriage was waiting for them. Harnessed to it were eight white wooden carousel horses, their manes painted on in golds and pinks and there were black-feathered headdresses attached to their halter.

'Wow,' Gerty said, as she grabbed Charlotte's arm in excitement. 'I used to love riding on the carousel horses when I was little.'

'How are those horses meant to get us anywhere, they aren't real?' Stef said.

Just then one of the horses near the front neighed loudly and moved its front leg that caused Stef to jolt backwards.

'Okay but I still don't know how we are all meant to fit in that, it's tiny,' Stef remarked, as she watched as some of the other girls climbed up the steps and into the carriage.

'Let's find out,' Charlotte pulled Stef forwards.

'I don't mind if you go first,' Stef said, as she let Charlotte pass her.

Charlotte nodded, before she walked up the steps and into the carriage. Inside was at least the same size as the grand hall and it was full of circular glass tables surrounded by gold and red padded chairs.

'Double wow,' Gerty said open-mouthed, as she walked in behind Charlotte.

Alice came in next, she was pulling on Stef's arm. They both stopped still when they saw inside the carriage, which caused the girl coming in behind them to walk straight into the back of Stef.

'Move it,' she growled.

'Sorry,' Stef muttered, as she and Alice walked over to Charlotte and Gerty, who were now sitting at one of the tables.

'This is cool,' Stef said.

'You weren't thinking that a minute ago when you were making excuses not to come in here,' Alice said.

'I was not, I just thought I'd forgotten my wand, that's all,' Stef blushed.

'At my old school we had this rickety old bus to take us on school trips. It constantly smelt of vomit and the springs from the seats dug into my back. This is definitely an improvement,' Charlotte said.

'I've never been on a bus, they sound awful,' Alice shuddered.

'They weren't so bad, well, apart from that school trip bus, that was terrible. Nothing like this though, this is amazing,' Charlotte said.

'My parents have a private chauffeur so I'm used to

transport that isn't overcrowded,' she looked around her at all the dressed-up girls sitting in the carriage. 'I suppose that this is passable.'

'Well I think it's amazing,' Charlotte said.

'Me too,' Gerty giggled. 'I can't wait, I've never been to a ball before.'

The carriage began to move and there were shouts of excitement between all the girls. The ball they had been anticipating since the beginning of term had finally arrived.

***

The Wizard's School was over the mountain range, disguised by a thick array of oak trees. The carriage passed under an arched gateway saying *Alexander's College*, and the magnificent brick castle came into view. Most of the girls jumped out of their seats and crowded around the windows, trying to get a glimpse of the castle.

The carriage came to a stop and Molly appeared by the door, her wand gripped firmly in her hand so that Charlotte thought she resembled a Gothic fairy.

'So, as you've all no doubt figured out, we're here. No pushing or shoving when getting off the carriage and if people near the front get off first that will make things easier. When you get outside wait in the yard with Sonya and Silvia for me and we shall lead you into the college.

Remember that just because you're out of the Academy doesn't mean that the code of conduct doesn't apply. If anyone rule breaks here it will be taken more seriously than it would be back at the Academy because you are representing it. This doesn't mean that you can't have a good time, just remember who you are and where you are,' Molly nodded to Sonya and Silvia and they stepped outside.

'Jasmine, you can start the line,' she pointed to a dark-haired girl in a black and white floral dress.

Ignoring what Molly had said some of the girls from the back tried to shove through the crowds, so that they could get out of the carriage before them.

'Watch it,' Stef said, as she got elbowed in the ribs.

Alice seemed to get pushed further back into the carriage, until she was almost at the back of it and then someone stood on the back of her shoe, causing her to lose her footing and step out of it. She had to wait until all the girls had passed her before she could put it back on.

'What's the rush?' Molly said, as she waved her wand and said the word 'Remitto.'

Instantly all the girls left in the carriage found that they could only move in slow motion.

'Now, those of you at the front go first,' Molly said.

The girls at the front slowly moved their way to the door, unable to move their arms and legs quickly.

'M-m-o-l-y,' a girl said as she passed her but on realizing that her words came out slowly too, she decided not to say anything else.

As soon as the girls stepped out of the carriage they went back to walking at a normal speed.

'Where's Alice?' Charlotte asked Gerty and Stef, as they stood outside. They'd managed to get off the carriage fairly quickly without getting shoved too much.

'Maybe she decided that the carriage is too common for her and she's waiting for her own personal chauffeur to collect her and drive her right up to the door,' Stef smirked.

'Stef,' Charlotte stared at her but failed to hide her smile.

'I was only messing.'

'There she is?' Gerty pointed over to a red faced Alice who stumbled her way down the steps of the carriage, followed by Molly. 'What happened to you?'

Alice went even redder, almost matching her shoes. She didn't reply to Gerty, instead she looked down at her feet.

'Do my shoes look okay?'

'Yes,' Stef rolled her eyes. 'If you like over-the-top sparkles, then they look great.'

'I meant they don't look damaged do they?'

'No,' Gerty crouched down and inspected them. 'They look perfect.'

'Follow me,' Molly shouted, as she walked past the girls.

The high ceilings and brick-walled corridors carried a medieval feel to them. There was a knight-of-armor by one of the walls and colorful eagle-crested banners, shields and crossing swords decorating the walls.

'It's like a fortress,' Gerty whispered to Charlotte. 'Do you think they had proper battles here back in the olden days.'

'Probably,' Charlotte replied.

Molly led them into a large hall, with disco lights and music playing. There were chairs lining the sides of the room and a large table filled with snacks, cups and a punch bowl. Also in the room were boys, some were dancing, some were at the refreshment table and some were siting on the chairs...but all of them stopped what they were doing and stared over at the girls as they entered.

Some of the older girls rushed over to certain boys and greeted them with hugs and smiles. There was a boy by the refreshment table, with floppy dark hair that was swiped across his forehead who winked over at Molly. She failed to hide her smile as she coyly looked back at him before looking away.

'Welcome, welcome to Alexander's,' a tall man in a black waistcoat and pinstriped trousers said as he took wide strides across the room.

'Ah Molly, I presume Miss Moffat is well?' he slightly lowered his head to her so that he wasn't towering over her as much.

'Alexander, yes she is very well and sends her regards.' Molly sounded so formal and grown up!

'It has been too long since I saw her last, we are so near yet it seems so far away. Running a school is very time-consuming.'

'Yes, I imagine it is.'

'Now, now, don't just stand there,' he turned to face the new girls who were still lingering in the doorway. 'Go and dance.'

'Let's get a drink and go and sit down somewhere,' Charlotte said to the others.

They made their way over to the drinks table and Gerty used the large punch bowl spoon to fill up four cups. With their drinks in hand they walked over to a row of empty seats and sat there awkwardly.

Some of the older girls were dancing with the boys, while most of the new girls and boys sat on opposite sides of the room, not knowing how to approach each other.

Demi seemed immune from first dance nerves, even without Margaret for company. She was already on the dance floor with a few girls from the year above, twirling in her leopard print skirt.

Charlotte looked across the room at the sitting boys, her gaze falling upon a brown-haired boy, with wide eyes and golden skin. He noticed her looking at him and she quickly lowered her gaze, her heart increasing in pace.

'We're at a dance, so we need to actually dance,' Gerty stood-up and pulled at Alice and Stef's arms. 'You too Charlotte, you're not getting out of it just because I'm out of arms.'

'Okay, okay,' Stef groaned, as she got to her feet.

Gerty led them over to the dance floor and began to sway in tune to the music. Stef swung out her arms and legs and Demi sniggered over at her.

'*Bonum saltator*,' Gerty flicked her wand out in front of Stef.

'What did you do to me?' Stef glared at Gerty.

'Try dancing now,' she smiled.

Stef began to dance and soon realized that she was in rhythm to the music, moving as a skilled dancer would.

'Go Stef!' Gerty wolf-whistled, as Stef danced around the dance floor.

A group of boys and girls saw Stef and began to clap and one boy with spiked dark hair walked over to her and began to dance with her. Demi stopped dancing and glared over at Stef, an annoyed look on her face.

'There's no way that Stef could dance like that without some help, what spell did you use?' Demi said, after she had marched over to Gerty, Charlotte and Alice.

'I don't know what you're talking about,' Gerty grinned.

'I don't believe you. It doesn't matter anyway because I'm far more advanced at casting spells than you are, you're just a kid,' she huffed, as she aimed her wand at herself and said *'Peritus saltator.'*

She smirked before she cartwheeled across the floor and then spun on the spot like a spinning wheel. When she came out of the spin she did a row of back-flips before she began doing some fancy dance moves across the room.

'Talk about overdoing it,' Gerty giggled.

'She's making me dizzy just watching her,' Charlotte said.

'The dance floor at home is far larger than this one, we throw a grand ball every summer. I suppose you can all come to the next one,' Alice said.

'Will there be cute boys there?' Gerty asked.

'There are a few boys our age that are invited with their parents that I suppose are okay.'

'It doesn't matter about the boys, we'd love to come,' Gerty smiled.

'That sounds great,' Charlotte said.

'That spell you used was good, look at Stef go,' Charlotte said to Gerty, as she pointed over at her still dancing with the boy on the dance floor.

It was then that Charlotte noticed three really great looking boys...standing there and smiling at her group. She looked down, feeling a little embarrassed.

When she looked up again, the cute browned-haired boy wasn't standing with his friends any more, instead he was walking across the room, his friends following him. At first she thought that they were going to the refreshment table but instead they kept on walking across the room towards her. Her pulse was thudding in her head and her hands started to sweat.

'Do you want to dance?' the shortest boy said to Alice. She blushed as she nervously nodded and followed him onto the dance floor.

The cute boy looked at Charlotte and gave her an awkward smile, he was just about to ask her to dance when Demi grabbed his arm as she danced past him.

'Dance with me,' she said, not giving him much of a chance.

The third boy stammered, 'Hi,' and then walked off, blushing.

'He was clearly about to ask you to dance,' Gerty sighed. 'That girl should find her own boy and not kidnap other peoples. She has ruined everything!'

'It was hardly kidnapping and he might not have wanted to dance, he might have wanted to ask me something else,' she looked over at the boy who was swaying uncomfortably next to Demi's exaggerated dance moves.

'He didn't go by choice, you should go over there and get him back.'

'No way,' she shook her head, before she looked over at him and saw that he was looking back at her.

Demi continued her wild dancing, her face looked exhausted but her body seemed unable to tire. She flayed her arms around and that's when she whacked the boy in the head with her elbow. He dropped to the ground with a thud and Charlotte raced over to him and bent down by his side. His eyes were shut and he wasn't moving.

'I didn't mean to hurt him,' Demi said worriedly, as she danced around the boy, unable to stop.

'I know Demi, just go and dance over there and give him some room,' Charlotte said, as she pointed across to the other end of the dance floor.

'Please, wake-up,' she whispered to him. 'You're too cute not to be okay.'

'Thanks,' the boy said, as he winked at her, before he pulled himself up into a sitting position.

Charlotte blushed and looked down at him awkwardly. They both smiled at each other and soon their smiles turned into laughter.

'Are you okay?' Alexander rushed over.

'Yes sir, a rogue elbow can't keep me down,' the boy replied.

'I'm glad to hear it,' he stretched out his arm and helped the boy up. 'I suggest you watch out for elbows and other limbs if you're considering asking this young lady to dance,' he looked over at Charlotte.

'I think I've had enough of dancing for one night,' he blushed. 'Any chance you want to sit down and talk for a bit?' he looked at Charlotte with his beautiful eyes and dazzling smile.

'Yes. Erm, I mean, yeah, that'd be great,' she spluttered out.

They walked side-by-side over to the chairs and sat down next to each other. For a few minutes they sat in silence passing smiles between each other.

'I'm Charlie.'

Charlie...So Handsome!

'Charlotte.'

'It's good to meet you Charlotte,' he smiled.

'You too.'

The music stopped playing and a loud horn sounded. All eyes fell on Molly who was standing by the refreshment table.

'Thank you to Alexander's College for hosting what I'm sure you'll all agree was a magnificent night?' there were cheers of agreement from the girls and some of the boys. 'All girls are to follow me outside to return back to the Academy. Make sure you've got all of your belongings, especially your wands,' she glanced a look at the dark-haired boy who'd winked at her earlier, before she led the girls out of the hall.

'I better go,' Charlotte said.

'I'll see you at the next dance,' he smiled.

'I'd like that.'

She stood-up and looked over at Gerty and the others who were waiting for her. She gave one last smile to Charlie, hoping that the next ball wouldn't be too long away.

'For the record, I think you're cute too,' he said.

Charlotte couldn't hide her grin, as she gave him a wave and joined the others. They all began following the other girls out of the hall.

'He's very cute,' Gerty giggled.

'He is, isn't he?' Charlotte smiled. She felt like she was walking on a cloud and butterflies were flying around her stomach.

'He's alright but Benjamin was cuter,' Alice said.

'Did Demi ever stop dancing?' Charlotte peered back at the empty dance floor.

'Who cares,' Stef said.

'Maybe she danced herself back to the Academy,' Gerty laughed.

'More like she got expelled for crimes against dancing,' Stef snorted.

'He had such lovely eyes,' Alice gave a thoughtful sigh. 'Like dark blue jewels, but not the cheap kind. They were as blue as the sapphire engagement ring my mother has.'

'You're see him again soon enough,' Gerty put her arm around Alice's shoulders.

'How could anyone resist those shoes,' Stef grinned.

'Do you think that's the only reason he liked me? I can't possibly wear the same pair twice,' Alice looked worried.

'He liked you for you, regardless of your sparkly shoes,' Charlotte said.

'Yes, you'll right,' Alice smiled.

'What was your boy like?' Charlotte asked Stef.

'He was okay,' she smiled.

'Just okay?' Gerty asked.

'Not, just okay, but okay,' she grinned.

'At the next dance I'll ask Charlie if he has a friend for you,' Charlotte looked at Gerty.

'Really?' Gerty said excitedly.

'Yep.'

'I can't wait,' she did a jig on the spot.

'Nobody ask Miss Maker for a beauty spell before the next ball,' Stef said.

'If she makes us do one, I'm not drinking it,' Gerty said.

'We don't need to ask her for dancing spells as Gerty has that one covered,' Charlotte grinned.

'Yeah, that spell was great and it really showed Demi up which is always a bonus.'

'Demi managed that all by herself,' Gerty said.

'I hope she's still dancing on the journey back, that'd make Molly so annoyed she'd probably turn her into a mouse,' Stef laughed.

'Home time,' Gerty sighed, as she looked over at the carousel horses and carriage.

Charlotte turned back and took in one last look at the castle, before she turned around and followed the others onto the carriage. It had been a magical night, one that she was sure she would remember forever.

Chapter Four

It was breakfast time and the grand hall was full of students, all talking amongst themselves as they grabbed fruit off the plants in front of them. Large black and white birds flew through the windows and dropped hard-boiled eggs into each of the eggcups in front of the girls.

Alice and Gerty placed their arms over their heads, worried that the eggs would hit them instead, but the birds didn't miss, nor did the eggs break.

'What shall we do today?' Gerty asked, as she cracked the top of her egg with her spoon.

It was Saturday so they didn't have lessons today, which meant an entire day of free time.

'It has to be inside the castle, no way am I going out in this weather,' Stef gestured to the window, drops of fierce rain were splatting against it.

'We could go to the games room,' Gerty said.

'I'm not playing bumblebee table tennis, my arm still hurts from where that thing stung me last time,' Stef said.

'You said that you were good at table tennis,' Gerty chuckled.

'Yeah, well I'd never played it with bumblebees for balls before.'

'I need to go to the library to study. If one of you could come with me that'd be great, as the Mistress of the Books always gives me funny looks since the Margaret thing. I don't like being in there alone,' Charlotte said.

'I'm not spending my free day in the library,' Alice remarked.

'I'll come with you,' Gerty said cheerfully.

'Who's that girl sitting with Demi,' Stef pointed over to the table near the door.

A pretty girl with shoulder length black hair was sitting opposite Demi.

'I've not seen her before, have you?' Gerty asked.

'No,' Stef said and both Charlotte and Alice shook their heads.

'She looks slightly older, maybe she's from the year above,' Charlotte said.

'Possibly, although I recognize most people in this place and I don't recall her at all,' Gerty said.

'It was only a matter of time before Demi replaced Margaret,' Stef shrugged.

'I guess, I just hope that she's nicer than Margaret,' Charlotte said.

'Everybody's nicer than Margaret,' Gerty grinned. 'Imagine someone meaner than Margaret, it doesn't bear thinking about.'

'Do you think Margaret's at the bad witch school?' Alice asked.

'I doubt even they would have her,' Stef snorted.

'I just hope she doesn't come back here,' Charlotte looked down at the remnants of her egg, recalling what it was like being a cockroach. 'Let's get out of here,' she pushed her chair back.

'Hang on,' Stef grabbed a few more pieces of fruit off the plant and popped them into her mouth. Then she grabbed a couple more and put them into her cardigan pocket, causing Gerty to give her a look.

'What, they're for later,' Stef replied.

They all glanced at Demi and the new girl as they walked past them. They were chatting to each other as if they'd known each other for years and they didn't seem to notice that anyone was looking at them. Charlotte found herself hoping that this girl was nothing like Margaret because they definitely didn't need a new one of those around.

***

Charlotte had spent the last few hours in the library with Gerty. The Mistress of the Books hadn't taken her eyes off her since they'd arrived, but that was to be expected. Charlotte didn't want to cause trouble, she just wanted to study and she hoped that the Mistress of the Books would eventually realize that.

Charlotte loved being at the Academy but she felt like she was miles behind everyone else because she hadn't grown up surrounded by magic. She kept up with the spells and potions in class but out of class she didn't know anywhere near as many spells as Gerty or Margaret did. That's why she was using her weekend to learn some spells and Gerty was a great help.

'This is a good spell,' Gerty whispered, as she moved the open book over to Charlotte.

'Spell blocker,' the book spoke quietly, so that Charlotte had to lean in closer to it to hear it. 'Aim your wand at the person who is casting a spell on you and as soon as they begin casting it flick out your wand and clearly say the word 'Prohibere.' This will block their spell.'

'Prohibere,' Charlotte said under her breath, before she wrote the word down in her notebook. 'Prohibere.'

'Shush,' the Mistress of the Books said, as she glared over at her.

Charlotte closed the spell book and sighed. She wanted to be able to learn spells without the fear of being turned into a toad or having her mouth sewn-up.

She continued to communicate with Gerty via hand signals, not daring to utter a word.

When they were finished in the library they put their books on the shelf by the door and were about to walk through it when Demi appeared with the girl from breakfast.

'Charlotte, Gerty, this is Destiny, she's new here and she'll be in our class,' Demi said.

Hey,' Gerty smiled.

'Hi,' Charlotte said.

'Shush,' the Mistress of the Books said to them.

'Demi's just showing me around, this place is so massive,' Destiny whispered.

'Shush,' the Mistress of the Books said again.

'We better go, it was nice to meet you,' Charlotte quietly replied.

The next thing she knew the Mistress of the Books had flicked her wand and Charlotte had shrunk down into a pale brown mouse.

'There is to be no sound in my library,' The Mistress of the Books said sternly.

Gerty bent down and rummaged around the pile of clothes and pulled out Charlotte, cupping her in her hands.

'Ew, get it away from me,' Demi squealed, as she jumped back.

Gerty held Charlotte in one hand and picked the pile of clothes up in her free hand and walked over to a table.

Eventually the Mistress of the Books strode over to the table and flicked her wand, causing Charlotte to change back into a human. She quickly reached for her clothes, as Gerty stood in front of her and tried to cover her from view of the other girls in the library.

'No more talking in my library,' she said sharply.

Both girls hurried out of the library and out of earshot of the Mistress of the Books.

'So much for that blocking spell.' Charlotte sighed and whispered, 'She will never like me.'

'I don't think using that spell on the Mistress of Mean would have been a good idea, she probably would have turned you into a slug for the entire weekend if you'd used that on her,' Gerty said.

'I know, it's just that I'm trying to learn new spells. It's hard to do that when I'm a mouse.' Charlotte smiled.

'I thought she said she turned people into toads?'

'Maybe she's turned so many people into toads she fancied a change,' Charlotte shrugged. Having to deal with an aggressive librarian was starting to get to her.

'Anyway, we'll have to develop sign language for when we're in the library,' Charlotte made exaggerated gestures with her hands.

'That might be a good idea,' Gerty chuckled.

'Come on,' Gerty grabbed Charlotte's arm. 'Let's go and find the others and tell them about Destiny.'

***

'It seems a strange time to start at a school, are you sure she wasn't just looking around?' Stef said, kicking her legs out behind her as she lay out on her bed.

'No, Demi definitely said that she was new here and in our class,' Charlotte said.

'If Demi said it, then it must be true,' Stef said sarcastically.

'I don't see why she'd lie about this, she introduced Destiny to us,' Charlotte said.

'Yeah and Charlotte got turned into a mouse by the Mistress of Mean for talking,' Gerty laughed.

'Really!' Alice said, as she peered up from the book she was reading.

'Yes, really,' Charlotte groaned.

'It was unfair, seeing as Charlotte hardly did any talking, it was mainly Demi.'

'It's my own fault that the Mistress of the Books doesn't like me, I shall just refrain from talking in the library again.'

'That's probably for the best, I prefer you human,' Stef grinned.

'I suppose there was an opening at the Academy now that Margaret's gone,' Alice said.

'We don't need a new Margaret though,' Stef said.

'She seemed nice,' Gerty said.

'She's friends with Demi, so she can't be that nice,' Stef replied.

'I suppose we'll find out soon enough,' Charlotte said, believing that no one could possibly ever be at bad as Margaret.

***

The weekend came to an end and a new week began. Destiny was at breakfast wearing her school uniform and chatting away to Demi. It seemed as though she was an official student at the school and the girls weren't sure what to think about this.

They were on their way to their class with the Mistress of Spells when Stef walked up alongside Destiny and Demi.

'What is she doing?' Alice asked Charlotte and Gerty.

'Being Stef,' Charlotte replied, as she walked over to Stef.

'Hi, I'm Stef, I see that you're new here?' she grinned at Destiny.

'I'm Destiny, Destiny Catslove, although I've already met some of you,' she smirked over at Charlotte.

'Squeak, squeak,' Demi giggled.

'It's a strange time for you to start here?' Stef enquired.

'I got expelled from my last school,' she shrugged.

'Really! What did you do?' Gerty asked.

'I was only messing around with a spell, they went wayyy overboard on their punishment,' she rolled back her eyes. 'My parents were furious, for the whole of the journey back they went on and on about the family name and how I needed to think about my actions, blah, blah, blah.'

'I'm Alice Smithers, from the well-known Smither's family. No doubt you've heard of us?' Alice said.

'No, I haven't. It's not my fault that school took itself too seriously. I wanted to go to Witchery College but my mom said, 'no respectable witch goes there,' she mimicked in a high-pitched tone.

'Why would you want to go there, they practice black magic?' Stef asked.

'Exactly, it's so frustrating being a witch and not being able to learn the spells I want to. Anyway, I'm stuck in this place now and I can't get expelled again as it's not worth the aggravation from my parents.'

'You're tall, how old are you?' Stef asked.

'Twelve, it was my birthday last week. Looks like that makes me the oldest, she looked down on the other girls, stopping on Gerty. 'And you're definitely the youngest,' she smirked.

'I was moved up a year,' Gerty said coyly.

'Gerty's a talented witch, she deserved to be moved up a year,' Charlotte said.

'Yeah, sure,' Destiny rolled her eyes. 'Anyway, see you in class,' she turned her back on the girls, grabbed Demi's arm and hurried her up the corridor.

'Why did you do that? Charlotte turned to Stef.

'What?'

'Go over and talk to her?'

'Why not?' she shrugged.

'Because she might be as mean as Margaret and she's already seen me be turned into a mouse.'

'She seems okay to me,' Gerty smiled.

'I suppose so,' Charlotte said under her breath, unable to trust her own words.

'I've never heard of her family before, so they obviously aren't as well-known as my family are,' Alice said.

'Come on, we have a class to get to,' Stef gave Alice a gentle prod in the back.

'I was already walking at an adequate speed, there's no need to prod me,' she struck out her arm to prod Stef back but she dodged out of the way.

'Can't catch me,' she grinned.

'Tribus *digitorum ictu*,' Alice flicked her wand at Stef.

'Ow!' Stef said, as she jumped forwards. 'Who did that?'

'Did what?' Alice smirked.

'Prodded me in the back. Ow, it happened again,' she glared at Alice.

'I don't know what you're on about,' Alice feigned concern as she hid her wand down by her side.

Gerty placed her hand over her mouth to try and disguise the fact she was giggling and Charlotte bit down on the side of her lip. There weren't many times when Alice got one back on Stef, so this was a rare occasion.

'Ah, make it stop,' Stef moaned, as an invisible force jabbed her arm. 'You guys suck,' she rubbed her arm and looked at

Gerty and Charlotte who were still struggling to hide their laughter.

'I don't see anything,' Alice said, keeping her composure.

'I'll get you back for this Alice Smithers, just you wait and see,' Stef grinned, before she began to laugh too.

They walked into class in good spirits and sat down at their seats. Miss Scarlet was sitting behind her desk, her hair as usual was elegantly pinned back.

'Quickly girls,' she said to the room and the rest of the girls hurried to their seats.

'I see we have a new girl in our class,' she smiled over at Destiny. 'So I shall briefly go over what I've told you before, no doubt some of you will benefit from the reminder. As you all know the *Book of Spells* is an ancient, extremely powerful book. Only I am allowed to touch it, but that doesn't mean that you won't be learning from it. You all have copies of the book but only I have the original, kept away where only I can see it.'

'Miss, how did you come to own it?' Stef asked.

'It was a matter of timing and having a pure heart. I like to think that the book was looking for me as much as I was for it.'

'Surely other witches and wizards want it too?' Demi asked.

'Indeed they do but they will have to make do with their copies. There are plenty of other spell books, most of them were written hundreds of years ago. I have some in here,' she gestured over to the large bookshelf at the far side of the room. 'And plenty more in my quarters. Collecting these books is a great pleasure of mine. We should all have pleasures and hobbies in life as they strive us onwards.'

Demi and Destiny giggled loudly and Miss Scarlet glared at them.

'I think Mistress of the Book's hobby is turning students into mice,' Charlotte whispered to Gerty.

'Some would say her main passion is books,' Miss Scarlet said and Charlotte blushed. 'Please refrain from talking in my class.'

Charlotte mouthed 'sorry miss,' as she lowered her head.

'Passion is what drives us forwards and causes us to thrive. Without passion succeeding becomes ever more difficult. One should never lose their passion. Now, all turn to page one-hundred-and-one in your books. Today we shall we practising a simple color-changing spell. As you can see there is an apple in front of each of you. With this spell you should be able to turn it from green to blue.'

'What's the point in a blue apple?' Alice said.

'It is merely a tool for you to practice with. Maybe if you put more thought into your spells instead of questioning instructions you would be more advanced at spells.'

Alice looked sheepish and Demi and Destiny continued to giggle.

'Will both of you please be quiet and concentrate on the spell at hand,' she stared at them.

They both stopped giggling and smiled at each other. Destiny waved her wand around in exaggerated movements that caused Demi to start giggling again.

Miss Scarlet flicked out her wand and a wart appeared on both of Demi and Destiny's noses. They both let out shrieks and covered their faces.

'Now make sure that you speak clearly when casting the spell,' she stood up and looked at the apple on her desk. '*Recensere azureus*.'

The apple immediately changed into a sky blue color.

'Cool,' a girl in the front row said.

'Can you eat it?' Patricia asked.

Miss Scarlet reached over and picked up the apple, bringing it up to her mouth and taking a moderate sized bite out of it.

'Delicious,' she gave a sly smile. 'The apple is still an apple, it is only the color that has changed,' she placed the apple back on her desk.

'It's important that you pronounce the spell clearly. Place your wands down on the table and repeat after me,' all the girls did as she asked, including Demi and Destiny who were still covering their faces. '*Re-cen-sere*.'

'*Re-cen-sere*,' the girls repeated in unison.

'*Az-u-re-us*.'

'*Az-u-re-us*,' they repeated.

'Good, good, one last time but this time we shall combine the words together. Re-cen-sere az-u-re-us.'

'*Re-cen-sere az-u-re-us,*' the class said.

'Wonderful, now let your passion show in your skills and turn that apple blue. There will be a prize for the person who excels the most.'

Miss Scarlet had made the spell look simple but it turned out to be more difficult than it looked. A girl near the back of the room managed to set her apple on fire and Destiny turned hers black instead of blue.

'*Recenere azueous*,' Stef said confidently. Her apple shook before it vanished. Huh, where's it gone?' Stef peered around for it. 'Who stole my apple? Demi, give it back.'

'It's not my fault you suck at magic, so I suggest you shift the blame back on yourself,' Demi sniggered, one arm still covering her face.

'It appears you said the spell wrong. Making an object disappear is no mean feat but it's not the spell we are practising. No doubt your apple will pop up somewhere in the Academy. I suggest you work on your pronunciation further.'

Charlotte had tried the spell twice already but nothing had happened. She looked over at the other girls' apples, noticing how Alice's hadn't changed and Gerty's was now a deep shade of purple, a fact she seemed proud of.

'*Recensere azureus,*' Charlotte said, as she flicked her wand out in front of the apple and watched with delight as it immediately turned to a sky blue colour.

'Brilliant work Charlotte,' Miss Scarlet said.

'Thanks,' Charlotte blushed.

Spell practice finished and all the girls sat back down in their seats and chatted amongst themselves.

'Silence,' Miss Scarlet said and the class fell quiet. 'Good effort was made by you all. To those of you who managed to master the spell, well done. To the others, keep on practicing and remember that clear pronunciation and saying the words with a determined force is important. You may think that all a witch needs to do is flick their wand around and utter a few choice words but I can assure you that spell casting is an art-form that requires practice and attention to detail. You must never give-up, nor must you ever take what we do for granted.

For successfully completing the spell first...the prize goes to Charlotte,' Gerty and Stef cheered and some of the other girls clapped. 'This is your reward,' she passed her a small vial full of a glittery silver substance.

'What is it?' asked Stef.

'Fairy dust, sprinkle it when you need some guidance and it will help you make your decision.'

'Cool,' Charlotte said under her breath, as she held the vial up to her face and studied it.

'It is of great importance that you only use it sparingly.'

'Thank you and I will,' Charlotte smiled, as she placed the vial down on the table.

'Miss, I was wondering, could you tell us more about *The Book of Dragons?*' Stef asked.

At first Miss Scarlet gave her an icy glare and Stef sank further down into her chair, worried that she was going to be turned into a toad.

'*The Book of Dragons* is strictly prohibited for young witches such as yourselves. It is dangerous to even the most powerful of witches and in the past has caused many problems. I advise you to keep away from this subject and to forget about this book,' she said firmly, her stern gaze seeming to fix on all of the girls at the same time.

'Right girls, first things first,' her tone was cheery as she waved her wand over at Demi and Destiny and the warts on their noses vanished. 'You better get off to your next lesson and remember a true witch never stops learning.'

Charlotte grabbed her books and her vial of fairy dust. She gave Miss Scarlet a smile and followed the others out of the door.

'I didn't know fairy dust was an actual thing,' Gerty said, as they left the room and walked up the corridor.

'You didn't know that fairies existed?' Stef snorted.

'Of course I did, I just didn't know that fairy dust was a thing, that's all.'

Charlotte didn't say anything, she didn't want to admit to them that until today she'd had no idea that fairies were real. When she was little she used to go down to the bottom of her garden where the plants bloomed in violets and yellows and she pretended that fairies lived amongst them. There was so much in the world that she hadn't known about and she felt like a novice.

'I've never seen fairy dust before,' Alice said and Charlotte held the vial up for her to see.

'What! You don't have a room full of it at home,' Stef grinned.

'No, we don't. As I just informed you, I've never seen it before.'

'Come on Stef, it's not like she baths in it or anything, Gerty giggled.

'I think Miss Scarlet would class bathing in it as using too much,' Alice replied.

'You'd end up looking like a glitter bomb,' Stef laughed.

'Maybe you should try that look at the next school dance,' Alice grinned.

'Perhaps,' Stef smirked.

They arrived back at their room and changed their books. Charlotte tried to think of a safe place to put the vial and decided to hide it in the draw under her bed, wrapped up amongst her clothes.

'When are you going to use the fairy dust?' Gerty asked.

'I don't know, I'm not really sure how it works.'

'I'm sure you'll just know when to use it, you're smart,' Gerty said.

'Thanks,' she smiled, deciding that she was going to save it until the time came when she knew that she'd really need it.

'It's a shame she didn't leave the warts on Demi and Destiny's faces,' Stef said, as she walked towards the door.

'They'd be walking around everywhere like this,' Gerty covered her face with her arms and paced up and down the room.

The other girls burst into laughter as they watched Gerty.

'Stop it, I can't breathe,' Charlotte said in-between laughter, as she clutched her stomach.

'What's so funny about this,' Gerty's muffled voice said through her arm, which caused them to laugh even more.

It was a full five-minutes before they eventually stopped laughing enough to compose themselves and leave for their next class, knowing that they'd have to walk extra quickly to get there on time.

Charlotte had arrived at this Academy clueless about magic and not knowing anyone. Now she had a vial of fairy dust in her draw and some of the best friends she could ask for. Better still Margaret had gone and hopefully they'd be no more surprise visits from her.

She knew that Miss Scarlet only awarded those she truly believed deserved it, which meant that Charlotte was improving at spells. She was a witch, it ran through her blood and she was going to keep on learning to be the best that she possibly could be.

Chapter Five

The girls trudged their way across the yard over to Miss Dread, who was balancing on her two hands, her legs bent over her shoulders.

'I hope she doesn't expect us to copy that position?' Gerty whispered to Charlotte and Alice, as she gripped her broomstick tighter. Miss Dread had told them at the end of their last lesson to bring their broomsticks today, but she wouldn't tell them why.

'Same, although it'd be funny to watch people try it,' Charlotte replied.

'I'm sure it's not that difficult,' Alice stopped walking and balanced on one leg. 'See, easy,' she said, before she began to wobble and grabbed onto Charlotte's shoulder to steady herself.

'I reckon you should keep on practicing,' Gerty giggled.

'Come on girls, stop dawdling,' Miss Dread shouted over to them.

They quickened up their pace and walked over to Stef, who was talking to Melody about what pets they were going to get when they were older.

'I want a fluffy cat and I'd put a spell on it so that it didn't malt all over my furniture,' Melody said.

'I want something more unique, like a bat. I'd call it Shade and let it live in my attic,' Stef replied.

'A bat, how ridiculous,' Alice snorted.

'Darlings, gather round,' Miss Dread said, as she flipped her legs over her head and landed on her feet on the ground. She stood-up, and turned around to face the girls.

'I've got an exciting lesson in store for you today. Come,

come,' she gestured for them to follow her. She led them across the yard and over to a grassy hexagonal area that had a basket in each of its corners.

'I hope we finally get to play Save the Princess,' Gerty said excitedly.

'I hope so, I'm great at it,' Stef said.

'You haven't started playing it yet?' Destiny sniggered. 'At my last school we started learning it on the first day of term.'

Charlotte looked from Destiny to the hexagonal field with a perplexed look on her face. She had no idea what Save the Princess was but she didn't want the others to know this, so she remained quiet as she focused her gaze on Miss Dread.

'Darlings, the time has come for you to learn how to play Save the Princess.'

'Yes!' Gerty jumped on the spot and everyone turned and stared at her. 'Sorry, I've just never played it before,' she replied coyly.

'It's good to have an interest in something darling, you need to channel that into the game,' Miss Dread looked at Gerty, before she turned her gaze across the rest of the girls. 'For those of you that aren't familiar with Save the Princess, it is to witches what hockey or football is to ordinaries. As you can see the game is played on a hexagonal base and on each of the six corners is a basket. You shall be split into two teams and your aim is to fly on your broomsticks and get a ball into each of the six baskets, whilst at the same time you need to try and block the other team from getting the ball in before you.

You shall start with the first basket,' she cartwheeled over to the first basket and put her hand against it. 'The first team to get their ball into this basket will be rewarded with a spell. A ghost shall appear and tell you what you've won.'

'A ghost?' Alice worriedly said.

'Yes darling, a ghost. It shall tell you a spell, it is wise to think carefully about when to use it as it can only be used once and it shall only last for five-seconds. When all the corners have been fought over then a tower shall rise in the middle,' she jumped into the middle of the hexagonal and gestured to the space before she darted out of it.

'Princeps *turrim*,' Miss Dread said, as she directed her wand towards the middle of the hexagonal.

The ground began to shake and Gerty grabbed onto Charlotte's arm. A large bricked tower rose out of the ground and kept on rising higher and higher. When it stopped, the top was only just visible.

'Your aim is to get this doll,' she pulled a princess rag doll from behind her back, 'to the top of the tower before the other team get their princess doll up there.'

'This is the part where the spells you won earlier become useful, although as I said before, you can only use them once so use them wisely.'

'If one player falls from the tower, then their whole team must return to the start line before their climber must restart their climb up the tower. Be warned that it is not as straightforward as it looks, as the tower will not make things easy for you.'

'It looks easy to me,' Stef whispered to Charlotte.

They saw a shape in the sky nearing them that soon came close enough for them to realize that it was Miss Firmfeather. She flew across the yard on her broom and landed down by Miss Dread.

'Hi girls,' Miss Firmfeather waved.

'Miss Firmfeather is here to assist me with assessing you all,' Miss Dread said.

'Assessing?' Demi asked.

'All we want is for you all to try your best,' Miss Firmfeather smiled, as she put her broomstick down and picked up an ancient looking telescope. Surely she wasn't going to watch up that closely!

'Darlings, let's begin,' Miss Dread looked over to the girls. 'Red team,' she pointed at Destiny. 'Black team,' she pointed to Demi. 'Red, black, red, black, red, black, red,' she pointed at the rest of the girls in turn as she gave them a team color.

'Prepare to be beaten,' Stef said to Charlotte and Alice, who'd been put into the opposite team to her and Gerty.

'I doubt it,' Alice replied.

'Come on darlings, you can do this,' Miss Dread clapped her hands.

The girls split into their teams, Miss Dread cast a spell to lower the castle and then the game began. The girls whizzed around the court, throwing the ball without much persuasion. Charlotte lowered her head just in time as Destiny lunged the ball at her.

'You were meant to catch it,' Destiny growled.

'Sorry,' Charlotte blushed.

The only sports Charlotte was used to were tennis and hockey, so this was new to her. She had only just learned how to fly a broomstick and now she had been put into a fast paced and skilled game. She wanted to give it her best, but she felt like a penguin out in the desert.

'Come on girls, focus,' Miss Firmfeather said, as Miss Dread jotted notes down in her notebook.

'Alice,' Patricia shouted, as she threw the ball at her. She looked up just in time and caught it, throwing it into the first basket before Stef had time to intercept her.

A transparent ghost of a man dressed in armor appeared in front of Alice and caused her to fly backwards until she was pressed against the basket.

'The spell you've won will send an icy chill down the opponent you choose to freeze at will, *duratus,*' the ghost said, before it vanished into the air.

'Good job Alice,' Miss Dread said, which caused Alice to smile widely.

'Beginners luck,' Stef quietly snorted.

Demi scored next, getting the ball in the second basket and then one into the third basket. When it came to this game she was fast on her broomstick and ruthless, flying straight at the opposite team with force until they had no choice but to move out of the way.

'Come on, that's not fair,' Melody said after Demi had shoved into her and snatched the ball out of her hands.

'That's the name of the game,' Miss Dread shouted. 'Darling, you must hold tightly onto the ball before you throw it.'

Destiny tried to get the ball off Demi but she threw it over to a blonde girl named Victoria before Destiny could grab it. Victoria leaned back to try and catch it and ended up bashing into Charlotte who lost her balance and fell off her broomstick. She bounced onto the field and sighed, before she lifted herself off and picked up her broom.

'Come on Charlotte, stop sitting around,' Alice shouted to her, after she'd thrown the ball over to another girl.

Charlotte brushed herself off before she got back onto her

broomstick and tried to regain her balance as she flew her way back around the court.

By the time the red team got their ball into the sixth basket Melody had grazed her knee and Destiny had a huge bruise on her arm from where Demi had shoved into her to get the ball. The tower rose up from the center of the court and two princess dolls, one with red hair and in a red dress and the other with black hair and in a black dress appeared at the base of it.

'Normally they'd be one climber per team but today you shall take it in turns so that I can assess you,' Miss Dread said, as she appeared up from her notebook. 'Demi and Melody can go first, the rest of you can use the spells but remember to cast them wisely. Also, don't forget that the tower has plenty of surprises in store for you. Also if you teammate falls then you have to return to your team start-line,' she gestures to a black and red line on the ground in front of the tower. 'And you can't move away or use any of the spells you've won until your climber is up and back on the tower.

Demi was the first to grab her doll and begin to climb up the tower.

'Go on Melody,' Destiny shoved her forwards.

'That's not fair, Miss Dread hadn't told us to start,' Melody grumbled, before she grabbed the doll and began the ascent up the tower.

'Don't forget about your spells,' Miss Dread shouted over to the girls on the ground, who were both stood in their teams looking clueless.

'Use the ice one, arhh, what was it?' Destiny said to her team.

'I know it,' Charlotte said, as she looked up at Demi, who was about a quarter of the way up the tower. She flicked out her wand in her direction and said '*duratus.*'

Demi instantly froze on the spot, unable to move at all.

'Melody, hurry up and pass her while she's frozen,' Destiny shouted up at her.

Melody nodded and she started to climb up the ladder of the tower as quickly as she could. She placed her hand onto the next rung of the ladder and that's when a pair of large stone hands appeared from either side of the tower and gave Melody a shove. She screamed out as she let go of the ladder and tumbled down onto the bouncy ground.

'Melody is out, Charlotte, you go next,' Miss Firmfeather said.

Charlotte tried to ignore her nerves, as she picked the princess doll off the ground by Alice and began to climb the ladder.

'You need to be quicker than that,' Destiny shouted. 'Demi's almost halfway up,' she pointed over to Demi who was now unfrozen and way out in the lead.

'*Gestat,*' Stef said as she waved her wand at Charlotte.

Charlotte's grip began to slip, as if there was slimy oil on her hands. She tried to grab on the ladder but she couldn't grasp it, then the princess doll slipped out of her hand and she found herself sliding down onto the ground.

She landed on her feet, embarrassed at how little progress she had made up the castle.

'That was a good use of a spell darling,' Miss Dread looked over at Stef.

'Thanks a lot,' Charlotte looked at Stef, unable to keep her stern look for long before it turned into a large smile.

'Sorry,' Stef grinned.

Destiny didn't wait for Miss Dread to tell her to climb, she raced forward and picked the doll up.

'I'll show you how it's done,' she said confidently, as she began to climb up the tower.

Demi was closer to the top of the tower than she was to the bottom and she was convinced that she was going to win. She quickly climbed onto the next step and then the next, then the snakes appeared through gaps in the tower wall, slithering around her arms and legs so that she became tied to the ladder.

'Do something,' she screamed down to her team.

'Erm, *dimissus*,' Stef flicked her wand up at the snakes. Her wand immediately flew out of her hand and hit her across the wrist before it flew over to Miss Dread.

'Stef, you can't use spells that you didn't win. You are disqualified so come and stand over here with us,' Miss Firmfeather said.

'Well I didn't know,' Stef muttered, as she glared at the ground.

'I thought you said you were good at this game?' Gerty grinned.

Demi managed to shake the snakes grip off and carry on up the tower.

'*Magna Pila*,' Charlotte shouted, as she waved her wand up at Demi.

She began to expand so that she resembled a ball with legs and arms sticking out of it. She was now too large to hold onto the ladder and she rolled all the way down the tower and landed in a heap on the ground.

'Good one,' Patricia patted Charlotte on the shoulder.

'Victoria, your turn,' Miss Firmfeather said.

Victoria grabbed the princess doll and stepped around the now shrinking, unhappy looking Demi before she began to climb up the ladder.

The tower began to violently shake, Victoria held on tightly to the ladder and leaned in close to the tower whilst Destiny struggled to hold her grip and soon found herself falling onto the ground. The red team let out sighs and groans, as they watched as the tower stopped shaking and Victoria continued her climb.

'I thought you implied that you were the best at this,' Alice snorted.

'Let's see you do better,' Destiny snarled, as she thrust the princess doll into Alice's hands.

'Okay, fine,' she couldn't hide the doubt from her voice, as she headed towards the steps.

'*Cito*,' Demi flicked her wand up at Victoria. She began to hurry up the ladder with super fast speed, becoming too fast for any arms or snakes that tried to grab her.

'Oh no, she's not far from the top,' Charlotte sighed. 'We have one spell left and so do they.'

'Well let's use it then,' Destiny pulled out her wand.

'No, not yet,' Charlotte reached out and lowered Destiny's wand.

Alice was surprising herself and the other girls, she climbed like a squirrel and weaved out of reach of the grabbing arms. She wasn't far behind Victoria and she was convinced that she was going to reach the top first.

'*Multum unguibus*,' Demi said, as she aimed her wand at Alice.

'Look out,' Patricia shouted but Alice was already aware of the spell and managed to dodge out of its way.

'That's not fair,' Demi moaned.

'Looks like you're out of spells,' Destiny smirked, as she goaded the other team.

Lips appeared near the top of the tower and green gooey gunk spewed out from them and covered Alice and Victoria. They both squealed out, Victoria was the first to lose her balance and fall down from the tower, while Alice managed to hold on.

'Yuck,' Alice said, as she stuck the princess doll under her arm and tried flicking the slime off her. 'It better not make my hair green!'

'Keep on going Alice!' Charlotte shouted.

Gerty ran up to Victoria, grabbed the doll off her and raced up the steps. Even though they were now slippery from the slime she still managed to get up them quickly.

'*Paulo genus*' Charlotte said, as she cast a spell at Gerty and hundreds of little spiders appeared and crawled over Gerty's skin.

'Good one,' Destiny said and Charlotte smiled.

'Ah, eek, eurgh,' Gerty shrieked but she kept on moving up the ladder.

Stone arms reached out and wrapped themselves around Alice. She tried to wriggle free from their grip but they were too strong.

'Hurry up Alice, she's about to overtake you,' Destiny shouted.

'You can do it Alice,' Charlotte said.

'Come on Gerty!' Stef shouted from her place over by the teachers.

None of the teams had any spells left so it was just the girls against the tower. Gerty overtook Alice and dodged the snakes that appeared through the tower gaps, as she made her way up to the top. Alice finally managed to escape the stone hands and hurriedly tried to catch up to Gerty.

The lips reappeared and more gloop flowed down the tower and covered the girls. Alice stopped and clung on tightly to the ladder until the slime had finished, but Gerty kept on going.

'Don't just stand there, move,' Destiny shouted up to Alice.

The gunk stopped and Alice continued to climb but she was too far behind Gerty now. Gerty placed the princess doll at the top of the tower and the black team all cheered.

'That's a black team win,' Miss Dread said.

'Great try girls,' Miss Firmfeather smiled.

'Now, the girls that didn't get to climb wait here, whilst the rest of you can go and sit over there,' Miss Dread pointed across the yard.

'Well done Gerty, you were great,' Charlotte said to Gerty, as she walked up alongside her. 'And sorry about the spiders.'

'Thanks and I forgive you. It was the most fun ever, I hope I get to do it again.'

'I had more slime over me than you did, look, you're barely covered,' Alice pointed at Gerty.

'That's not exactly true,' Charlotte said, as she looked at Gerty's slime-drenched arms, hair and clothes. 'Gerty looks like a slug.'

'You can be a slug too,' Gerty giggled, as she tried to wipe some slime off her arm onto Charlotte, who managed to dodge out of the way in time. They both laughed as Gerty chased after her.

'So immature,' Alice said under her breath, before she glanced up longingly at the top of the tower and let out a sigh.

After all the girls had attempted the princess tower they all gathered around Miss Dread and Miss Firmfeather. Miss Moffat and Molly were now also there, which made Charlotte feel extra nervous.

'Well done girls, although you all got off to an interesting start you all showed great promise and greatly improved. We are yet to decide upon a final team but we can announce who the climber will be. Well done Gerty, you shall be the climber,' Miss Dread looked directly at her.

'Me?' she pointed her thumbs inwards to herself, a surprised look on her face.

'Yes, you are the best witch for the job.'

'Thank you!' she squealed, as she excitedly grabbed onto Stef's arm, covering her in slime.

'Gross,' Stef wiped the slime off her arm as she stepped away from Gerty.

'Sorry,' she grinned.

Alice folded her arms and sighed loudly as she looked away from Gerty.

'Alice, you shall be the substitute climber,' Miss Dread kept her gaze down at her notebook as she spoke.

'Well done Alice,' Charlotte said.

'Yeah, well done,' Gerty smiled.

Alice didn't reply, instead she sighed again, although she couldn't hide the faint smile from her face.

'You are all to report here for Save the Princess training on the dot at sunrise,' Miss Dread's words were followed by groans from the girls. 'It's going to be a tough week but practice makes perfect, I know you can all do it. Oh and darlings, don't forget your broomsticks.'

'My Academy has an excellent reputation when it comes to Save the Princess. We have won many trophies and had students go on to play professionally. Of course it is satisfying to win, but it is more important to know that you've tried your best and that you've played fairly and in the spirit of the game,' Miss Moffat said, as she glanced over the girls with her intense dark eyes.

She gave them all a slight smile before she nodded at the teachers and Molly before flew off on her broom.

'Remember darlings, bright and early tomorrow morning,' Miss Dread said cheerfully. And don't be late,' she added sternly, before she gave them all a wave and walked off with Miss Firmfeather.

'Bye girls, remember to fly smoothly and remain in control of your brooms,' Miss Firmfeather turned and said to them.

'Can we go now?' Stef asked Molly.

'First I want you to all gather around me,' she beckoned them forwards, until they were huddled closely together. 'By all means play fairly, but the girls from Witchery College tend to to be a little darker in their approach and may not

82

play nicely,' she whispered. 'Anyway girls I'll catch you all later,' she walked away from the girls and up the yard, her clipped up hair bouncing as she moved.

The girls gave each other confused looks before they dispersed and left the yard to go back to their rooms.

'What did Molly mean?' Stef said to her friends.

'I don't really know,' Charlotte replied.

'It's exciting, although my legs are really sore right now,' Gerty bent down and rubbed her legs.

'Well I'm glad I'm not the climber when we are against Witchery College as they might cask a dark spell on me,' Alice said.

'You can't use spells you didn't win remember,' Charlotte said, shaking her head. Sometimes Alice really got on her nerves with her negative comments.

'I'm sure it'll all be fine and they'll stick to the rules of the game,' Gerty was unable to hide the slight doubt from her voice.

'It'll be fine Gerty, besides you were amazing climbing up that tower. You were like the lizard that I saw run up a building when I was on holiday with my parents once.'

'Gerty the gecko,' Stef chuckled.

'I suppose you were okay,' Alice said.

'Thanks guys,' Gerty smiled.

'And Miss Dread looked at you when she said your name which is a first, usually we just get called *darlings*,' Stef mimicked Miss Dread's voice on the last word.

Alice gave an annoyed look as she looked away from the rest of the girls, recalling to herself how Miss Dread hadn't looked at her when she'd announced her as substitute climber.

'You guys do stink though,' Charlotte said, as she looked from Gerty to Alice. 'You can both have first dibs on the bathroom.'

'I think we need it,' Gerty wiped some slime off her arm and studied her fingers. 'Alice, you can use the bathroom first.'

'I am the one who is covered in the most slime. If this ruins my expensive tracksuit, then I'm sending the Academy the dry-cleaning bill.'

'I wonder if there's a spell for removing slime?' Charlotte asked.

'Probably, there's a spell for most things. It might come in useful to find out what it is as I have a feeling this isn't the last time I'll get covered in it,' Gerty grinned.

The fitness lesson had been tiring, messy and intense but Charlotte decided that compared to tennis and hockey it was by far the best sport there was. The thought of playing it again made her both excited and nervous at the same time. She hoped that she'd make the team because she enjoyed casting the spells, but she knew that she needed to improve her flying skills for her to stand a chance of making the team.

Chapter Six

The next week bought with it plenty of Save the Princess practice. Not only were they training at sunrise everyday but Miss Dread had decided to increase this to an extra practice before dinner as well. All the girls were tired and their limbs ached but they had also made vast improvements.

It was after their last practice before their match against Witchery College and all the girls were sat in a semi-circle in the yard around Miss Dread and Miss Firmfeather. They only had a morning practice today as Miss Dread wanted them to have time to recuperate before their match tomorrow.

'Darlings, you all did superbly today. Gerty, you're a natural climber,' Miss Dread smiled, as she looked down at her notebook. 'If you don't make the final team then you shall be on the sub-line which is just as important as playing, because you shall remain part of this team. Because of this you all need to keep your fitness levels up and you all must continue to attend practice on time.The team list for your first match is as follows: Gerty as climber.'

Stef and a few of the other girls cheered and Gerty grinned.

'I don't know why you're cheering when we already knew that,' Alice said.

'The rest of the team are Demi, Destiny, Patricia, Stef, Alice, Victoria and Charlotte.'

'We made it,' Stef gave Charlotte a high-five. 'I knew that we would.'

'I knew that I'd be playing, I am the substitute climber after-all. I need to get the feel for a proper game, rather than having my talents wasted sitting on the sub-line,' Alice added.

'Big-headed much,' Stef rolled her eyes.

'You're just jealous because you're not the substitute

climber,' Alice huffed, rolling her eyes.

'I know that you can all succeed darlings. You have all trained hard and I am proud of every single one of you girls. Now darlings go and shower then get some breakfast and I'll see you here tomorrow for the match. Remember that we don't give up at this Academy and you all need to trust yourselves darlings, because you can do it. Now go,' she shooed them with her hands. 'Before I make you do extra practice,' she chuckled.

The girls stood up quickly and hurried away, believing that Miss Dread probably would make them do extra practice if they lingered there for too long.

'At least two of our team are good players,' Demi said loudly to Destiny, as they walked past the others.

'Erm, we're all good players else we wouldn't have made the team,' Stef replied.

'If you say so,' Demi said and both her and Destiny sniggered.

'I'm so excited,' Gerty smiled.

'Yeah, me too,' Charlotte chewed on the side of the lip.

Charlotte was pleased that she'd made the team but she was also nervous at the thought of playing against Witchery College. She'd heard so many stories about them, most of which were bad. Worst of all she was afraid that the rumors about Margaret now attending Witchery College were true and that tomorrow she'd be face-to-face with her once again.

***

It was a placid afternoon and the girls were standing in the yard, dressed in team kits that they'd found laid out on their beds after their morning practice. They consisted of a pleated black skirt and a white t-shirt with the crossed wands crest and 'Miss Moffat's Academy' written on the back of them in black font.

Miss Moffat, Miss Dread and Miss Firmfeather were standing next to a broad shouldered woman who wore black shorts and a burgundy top with the word 'referee' written on the front and back of it. As she spoke to the teachers she fiddled with the whistle that was hanging from her neck.

Rows of tiered seats were now placed around the court and most of the seats were filled by the other teachers and students who were chatting excitedly amongst themselves.

'That cloud over there doesn't look good, I hope it doesn't rain as it will frizz up my hair,' Stef pointed at the black cloud that was in the otherwise clear sky, before she continued to stretch her arms behind her back.

'I think it's moving closer,' Gerty said, as she stretched out her legs one at a time.

'Yeah, it definitely is.'

'They better cast a rain-cover spell, or else I'll end up with a cold for the next week,' Alice moaned.

The black cloud seemed to be moving closer towards them, it's speed increasing and with it the sky began to darken. Stef and Demi both placed their hands over their heads in preparation for the rain.

'It's not a cloud,' Destiny sniggered. 'Look,' she pointed up at it.

The black cloud was nearly upon them, only Destiny was right, it wasn't a cloud at all but instead it was a group of witches on brooms surrounded by a fleet of bats.

'Why do you still have your hands over your head?' Alice asked Stef.

'I don't trust them not to turn into an actual rain cloud or something,' she replied, not moving her hands.

A beautiful witch in a long black dress and a shawl made of glossy black feathers was the first to land, closely followed by the students, who were dressed in all black. Charlotte scanned her eyes over the girls in search of Margaret but she couldn't see her there.

'Look, her hair, she's got feathers,' Gerty whispered to Charlotte.

Charlotte looked at the woman and that's when she realized that Gerty was right, her hair was a thick mass of shiny black feathers, just like a ravens.

Most of the girls looked around the same age as the first
years, besides a couple of girls who were older. They weren't
dressed in the team sports kit like the others but instead
wore short black skirts and fitted black blouses with the crest
on the right side of it, the words 'Witchery College' written
below it. The older girl with dark skin and braided hair
glared over at Molly and Charlotte noticed how Molly

clutched tightly onto her wand as she gave her a stern look back.

Miss Moffat walked over and greeted the feather-haired woman with an awkward hug before she led her and her team over to the court.

'Come on darlings,' Miss Dread walked over to them. 'And don't forget to suck it up girls. I know that you can all do this, so don't you dare quit.'

'Why would we quit?' Stef whispered to Gerty, as they followed Miss Dread over to the court.

'Are you okay Charlotte?' Victoria asked Charlotte, on seeing how pale she'd gone.

Charlotte nodded, too nervous to speak. She clutched onto her broom tightly for support and looked over at the Witchery College girls who were sniggering over at them.

Miss Moffat and Mistress walked out into the middle of the court and all eyes fell on them.

'To those of you that don't already know, this is Mistress Ravenshawk, the principle of Witchery College. On behalf of my Academy, I welcome her and her students and hope that their time here is enjoyable,' Miss Moffat addressed the crowd.

'Thank you Miss Moffat,' Mistress Ravenshawk said, her voice soft but still managing to carry with it a strong sense of authority. 'It is an honor to be here for what I'm sure will be a pleasurable game. I'm sure it won't be long before we return the favor and have you back over to our grounds.'

'May the games begin,' Miss Moffat shouted and leprechauns appeared either side of the court and blew their trumpets loudly.

Both teams jogged a lap of the court, whilst the onlookers clapped and cheered. When they'd finished they both gathered in their teams and the referee walked over to the sideline of the court.

'Girls, I'm in no doubt that you can do this,' Miss Firmfeather smiled. 'Remember to stay focused, hold tightly onto your broom and remember how important timing is with the ball, don't let go of it too early or too late.'

Mistress Ravenshawk had her team gathered in tightly around her as she quietly spoke to them, making sure that no one else heard them.

Miss Moffat and Molly appeared in front of them and Miss Firmfeather nodded at the girls before she walked over to the referee.

'Witchery College are a formidable team but I believe in you and I know that you will give it your all. I want you all to do your best and most importantly...enjoy yourselves. It is important that you don't forget that you're representing this Academy, so show team spirit and give it your greatest effort. I'm far too nervous to stand here and say anything else, so I'm going to leave you all with Molly and go and take my seat,' Miss Moffat said, before she quickly walked across the court.

'Good luck girls and you better win or I'll turn you all into toads,' Mistress Ravenshawk winked, as she gave her team a wave as she followed Miss Moffat over to the reserved seats on one of the lower rows.

'I'm so nervous I think I may throw-up,' Gerty muttered.

'You'll be fine, just don't fall,' Destiny patted her on the shoulder, a confident look on her face.

'We'll be fine, those girls look ghastly, look at how ugly they all are,' Demi gave the other team, a large false smile.

Charlotte didn't say anything, instead she kept her gaze directed at the ground and hoped that she didn't look as nervous as she felt. Her arms were shaking and she tried gripping harder onto her broomstick so that no one noticed this.

'Are you okay?' Gerty whispered to her.

'Yeah, just nervous,' she whispered back.

'Miss Moffat's right, we just need to go out there and enjoy ourselves. Whatever happens, we've trained super hard and we just have to do our best,' Gerty smiled.

'Gather in,' Molly gestured them forwards. 'Miss Moffat's words contain a fine sentiment and all...but we are here to win. There's no way that you can lose against Witchery College,' she shuddered. 'My advice would be to play then at their own game,' she winked. 'You have to win or I might do some toad changing myself,' she smirked.

'No pressure then,' Stef rolled her eyes, before she followed Demi and Destiny out onto their starting positions on the court.

Charlotte stood in front of the third post by the side of a scary looking girl from Witchery College. Not only was she a good few inches taller than Charlotte, she also hadn't stopped snarling at her since they'd both taken their positions.

Gerty was standing in the middle of the court next to Witchery College's Climber. She was all smiles as she looked over at Charlotte and gave her a thumbs-up. The referee walked over to them and magicked up a large toad, half of it was orange and the other half was blue.

'Which color do you choose?' the referee said to the climber from Witchery College.

'Blue,' she replied without hesitation.

'Miss Moffat's Academy, you're orange. The side that the toad lands on first gets the ball,' she said, before she threw the toad high up into the air.

Both teams watched as the toad fell down onto the ground, its blue legs touching down onto the ground before it bounced back up.

'Blue it is,' the referee handed the ball to the Witchery College's smirking climber.

'Mount your brooms and wait for the whistle,' the referee watched as all the girls got onto their broomsticks and then she placed the whistle in her mouth.

The whistle blew and both teams flew up into the air and wasted no time in flying around the court. The Witchery College girl with the ball threw it over to the tall girl. Charlotte tried to intercept the girls catch but ended up being elbowed out of the way, only just managing to keep balanced on her broomstick.

Destiny snuck up behind the girl with the ball and snatched it out of her grasp. She flew away from her before she threw the ball over to Demi who then managed to get it past the Witchery College girl and into the basket.

There were loud cheers from the girls and the crowd and snarls and groans from the girls from the opposing team. The ghost appeared and floated in front of Demi and all the girls listened to what spell it was going to give her.

'Kittens are as sweet as honey, apart from their fur-balls as they aren't funny. Fur-ball overload with *fur-pila.*'

Charlotte made a mental note of the spell as she watched the ghost vanish. The game continued and Witchery College whizzed around the court, bashing into the girls brooms and grabbing the ball out of their grasps. Miss Moffat's team took the aggression well, remaining on their brooms and grabbing for the ball when they saw the opportunity.

Although Miss Moffat's team were trying their best Witchery College won the next two baskets, mainly because of the tall girl who kept a firm grip on the ball whilst still managing to swipe her broomstick and her elbow into the opposition.

Stef had the ball but Witchery College were closing in on her and she couldn't fly free.

'Alice,' she shouted, before she threw the ball over to her.

Alice reached out and caught it in one hand and the onlookers cheered excitedly from the side-line. A girl with her hair tied into bunches flew with speed towards Alice, trying to grab at the ball. Alice, ducked out of the way and threw the ball into the air, it spun over to the third basket and bounced against it. Charlotte held her breath as she watched the ball slow down it speeds and wobble from side-to-side before it tipped into the fourth basket.

The crowd cheered loudly and Alice grinned widely.

'As an eight-legged creature, you'll scuttle as you move. Accuracy and speed is what you have to prove, *Stilio crura,*' the ghost announced, before he disappeared.

A girl from Witchery College shoved Demi off her broom to claim the fifth basket.

'That wasn't fair!' Demi said with disgust. 'That basket shouldn't count!' she stared at the referee but got no reaction.

'Go on Miss Moffat's,' someone shouted from the crowd.

'Let's do this,' Stef said, before the referee threw the ball into the air and she charged forwards for it, managing to swerve out of the way of one of the opposing girls with such force that it caused them to topple off their broom.

Stef reached out her hands and grabbed it just before the girl with bunches could. There were more cheers from the crowd, blocking out the disgruntled snarls from the Witchery College girls.

Stef whizzed her way over to the sixth basket, weaving her way around the opponents. Suddenly the grass beneath her rose up like snakes and wrapped itself around Stef's arms, legs and broomstick. She shrieked out as the ball dropped out of her hand and onto the ground. The grass roots let go of her suddenly and she toppled down onto the ground, her broomstick landing on her leg with a thud.

Stef grabbed her broomstick and pulled herself up, but one

of the Witchery College girls had already grabbed the ball.

'They used an illegal spell,' Molly shouted over to the referee but she ignored her and stared out at the court...a smiling, dazed look on her face.

Mistress Ravenshawk gave a sly smile as she discreetly lowered her wand. She was adamant on her team winning and fair didn't come into it.

Charlotte saw the girl with the bunches putting away her wand, she knew that she'd cast the illegal spell on Stef and wondered why the referee hadn't disqualified her for it.

The girls tried to get to the ball back but the Witchery College girls were on full defence, swatting away anyone who got in their way. The last basket was scored and groans filled the stands and the court.

'They cheated!' Destiny said, as she flew over to the referee. 'Didn't you see the grass grab at Stef, that last basket should have been ours!'

The referee didn't reply, instead she gave a large smile and rocked her head in time to an unheard tune.

An annoyed Destiny went over to her team, who were being pep-talked by Miss Dread.

'Darlings, I know you can do this. You have won some excellent spells so don't waste them, stay strong as a team, communicate and Gerty, climb as if your life depends on it.'

'What is wrong with the referee?' Stef asked, as she rubbed her bruised leg.

'It seems as though foul play is afoot which gives you girls more reason to beat them. If you win by cheating then you haven't properly won, you have to rise above them and prove that you're the better team. Now drink your pumpkin juice as you must hydrate and remember to suck it up, as I know you can all do it,' she nodded at them, before she back-flipped her way back over to Miss Firmfeather who was attempting to communicate with the referee to no avail.

'It doesn't look like the referee will be of any use,' Charlotte sighed.

'Whoever cast that spell on the referee must have been super powerful,' Gerty said.

'Aren't you worried? If they cast that spell on Stef, imagine what they might cast on you when you're trying to climb that tower,' Alice said.

'Nah, what happens, happens. All I can do is try my best which is what I'm going to do,' Gerty shrugged, as she skipped her way over to the middle of the court where the castle had risen up.

'I hope that I come out of this alive,' Patricia said to Charlotte as she walked past her.

Charlotte bit down on the side of her lip as she walked over to the starting position. This morning she had been terrified that Margaret would show up, but instead she was equally as afraid of the other Witchery College girls. She wasn't about to give up though, if Gerty was willing to climb up that high tower knowing that any number of spells could be cast upon her, then Charlotte knew that she could try her hardest to help her from the court ground.

Miss Firmfeather blew the referee's whistle to signal the start of the tower run and both the tall girl and Gerty raced over to their dolls and began to climb their sides of the tower.

Gerty was ahead of the other climber, dodging and weaving away from the towers grabbing hands as she went higher and higher with no signs of tiring.

'*Tempestatis nubes*,' one of the Witchery College girls cast a spell up at Gerty and a storm cloud appeared over her head and drenched her.

This didn't deter Gerty who continued to climb at a fast speed. Charlotte looked up and saw how close Gerty was to the top of the tower and then she looked over at the opposing climber who wasn't far behind her. She met the eye of Demi and Stef for approval before she flicked out her wand at the Witchery College climber.

'*Fur-pila*,' she shouted and the climber stopped on the spot, bent over and began to cough out large balls of fur.

'Gross,' Stef chuckled.

'Go Gerty,' Charlotte cheered.

'*Arma*,' the girl with the bunches said and Charlotte's wand flew out of her hand and spun over to the stands.

Charlotte rushed after it, dread filling her body at the thought of it breaking. As she neared the stand Molly stood-up and pulled Charlotte's wand from behind her back.

'I told you that they didn't play fair,' Molly whispered.

'Thank you, thank you so much,' Charlotte gave a relieved

sigh, as she took her wand off Molly and raced back onto the court.

Gerty had managed to dodge two of the Witchery College spells and was now only a couple of steps from the top. She had her princess doll outstretched and her team was cheering excitedly.

Mistress Ravenshawk twitched her nose and said something under her breath as she subtly pointed up at Gerty.

'Honk, honk,' Gerty said as her hands and feet turned into flippers and she slid all the way to the bottom of the tower, the princess doll landing on her head.

'What happened?' Charlotte rushed over to her.

'How could you let that happen, you were an arm's reach away from winning,' Demi grunted.

'Honk, honk,' Gerty held out one of her flippers.

'They're nothing but a bunch of cheaters, let's beat them,' Stef pulled Gerty up onto her flippers.

The tall girl had almost reached the top of the tower and Molly was not impressed. She took out her wand and muttered out an incantation, smirking to herself as the tall girl instantly blew up so that she resembled a balloon and floated away from the tower, screaming out in a rage as she flew away.

'This is an outrage,' Mistress Ravenshawk stood-up and abruptly strode over to the referee. 'They clearly just used an illegal spell, do something?'

The referee grinned at her before she spun in a circle and then tipped her head from side-to-side. Mistress Ravenshawk huffed before she walked off, her feathered-hair blowing slightly in the breeze.

Mistress Ravenshawk looked over at Gerty whose arms and legs were back to normal and she had picked up the princess doll and was running towards the tower. She struck out her wand in a swift movement and the grass beneath Gerty's feet turned into thick, wet concrete. The faster Gerty tried to run, the further she sank into it.

Gerty was stuck and the concrete continued to move out across the rest of the Miss Moffat's girls until all of them were also stuck.

'What now?' Stef shouted.

'We have one spell left, the spider one,' Charlotte said.

'Then let's use it now,' Demi said, as she readied her wand. She tried hard to pull the spell from her mind but she couldn't remember it.

'*Stilio Crura,*' Charlotte said firmly, as she waved her wand over at Gerty.

Gerty began to shake before eight long furry legs sprouted out of her side, pulling her human legs out of the wet concrete and scuttling across it.

'Go Gerty!' Stef shouted, as she watched Gerty reach the tower and crawl her way up it.

The climber from the opposing team had deflated and was now at a similar point on the tower as Gerty was. Feathers came out of the holes in the tower and tried to tickle Gerty off but she didn't let go of her grip.

One of the tower hands grabbed the opposing climber and nearly swiped her off it. She steadied herself just as gunk poured from the lips that appeared near the top of the tower and covered them both. Gerty had a minor slip but soon recovered whereas the other climber lost her footing and only just rebalanced her grip in time.

'Velox scanders,' a short girl with freckle covered cheeks from the opposing team shouted, as she flicked her wand up at her climber.

The spell was meant to make her climb very fast but the girl had cast it wrong, causing their climber to move quickly the wrong way down the tower.

Her team yelled at her and Mistress Ravenshawk appeared at the sideline and once again attempted to argue with the referee.

'Go on Gerty!' Charlotte shouted.

'Keep on going!' Demi screamed.

Charlotte held her breath as Gerty made the last few steps and then stretched out her arms, placing the princess doll safely on top of the tower.

Loud cheers erupted and all the Academy girls hugged each other, including Demi who excitedly grabbed Charlotte into an embrace before awkwardly letting go of her.

'We did it,' Stef cheered, as she patted Alice on the shoulder.

'Of course we did, I'm from the type of family that does not know how to lose!' she replied.

'Foul,' the girl with bunches shouted over at the referee. 'They cheated so we should win.'

'We did not cheat,' Demi marched over to her. 'You're just a sore loser.'

'The game should be rerun!'

'No chance!' Demi replied.

Mistress Ravenshawk looked frustrated as she walked across the court over to the tall girl, her wand at the ready.

Charlotte thought that she was going to turn her into a toad but instead she thrust the girl's broomstick at her and said something that Charlotte couldn't quite hear.

The Witchery College team were either crying or shouting at Miss Moffat's Academy team and spells were flying between the two sides.

The girl with bunches was now clucking and walking about like a chicken, much to Demi's amusement and Patricia had been turned as blue as a blueberry.

Molly was in a heated debate with two of the older girls from the Witchery College and although outnumbered, Molly didn't look in the slightest bit concerned. She managed to turn both of the girls into grey rats before they had a chance to cast a spell on her. Molly grinned as she stepped over them and their pile of clothes as she walked off to join the girls on the court.

The tall girl was glaring at Charlotte, her wand raised. She was about to use the blocking spell that Gerty had found for her when she saw Miss Moffat flick her wand.

Calmness ascended on the girls and all the cast spells reversed. Both the tall girl and Charlotte lowered their wands and walked over to their teams.

Miss Moffat walked into the center of the court where the tower had now been lowered and she coughed loudly to clear her throat. All attention turned to her and the yard fell silent.

'Congratulations Witchery College on your superb effort and thank you for travelling over to our Academy. It was a pleasure to host you and to see you play strongly. Now, my girls, you showed that strong will and exquisite teamwork will pay off. I am very proud of you all and there will be a special celebration for you on the weekend.'

Miss Moffat nodded over at Mistress Ravenshawk who nodded back, the furious look still on her face.

'Come on girls, let's go,' Mistress Ravenshawk clapped her hands loudly and her broomstick appeared by her side.

All of the Witchery College girls flew over to Mistress Ravenshawk, including the two older girls that were now human but were still twitching erratically.

They all glared and growled in the direction at the other girls as they took off up into the air and flew off, a mass of bats surrounding them.

'We did it,' Gerty wrapped her arms around Charlotte and Alice.

'If you've got slime on my clothes then you can wash them,' Alice replied, although she didn't move away.

'But it isn't one of your expensive tracksuits?' Gerty giggled.

'I still don't want it to get dirty.'

'We couldn't have done it without you Gerty, you're a natural climber,' Charlotte said.

'Eek, we won,' Gerty ran on the spot.

'I wonder what the celebration will be?' Charlotte asked.

'I hope there will be cake there,' Stef said.

News of their win had spread and as they walked back to their rooms every student congratulated them.

'I could get used to this, it's like being famous,' Stef said, as she pushed their bedroom door open.

The others followed her into the room and the doors of the large ornate wardrobe immediately opened and sucked their broomsticks out of their hands.

'Mistress Ravenshawk didn't look very happy, do you think she'll turn her girl students into toads?' Gerty chuckled.

'I hope she does, they deserve it after cheating. I would have scored that sixth basket if it wasn't for their illegal move,' Stef said.

'Do you know why her hair is made of feathers?' Charlotte asked and Gerty shook her head.

'I know why, my mother told me,' Alice said.

'Do you really know?' Stef asked.

'Of course I do, my great-grandmother attended school with her.'

'Please tell us Alice,' Charlotte begged.

'Okay then,' Alice sat down on the edge of her bed. 'Many years ago Mistress Ravenshawk attended this Academy, only she wasn't known by the name Ravenshawk then, her name was Celeste. She was a powerful witch but she was disobedient and chose her desire to win at all costs, over loyalty. There was a witch called Roxanne who was also very powerful and Celeste was jealous of her.'

'Was Roxanne your great-grandmother?' Gerty asked.

'Of course not,' Alice said snootily. 'Anyway Celeste was so jealous that she used a spell from the *Book of Dragons* to take away Roxanne's powers. It just so happened that Roxanne's father, a man called Lord Adogold was one of the most powerful wizards in the world. When he found out what Celeste had done to his daughter he was furious. He hunted her down and although she was a strong witch...her powers were no match for him. He turned her into a raven and for many years she flew around the skies unable to turn herself back.

One day Lord Adogold decided that she'd paid the price for her actions and he turned her back into a human. He kept the feathers growing from her scalp so that she would remember never to dare cross him or his family ever again.'

'How do we know you didn't just make that up?' Stef said.

'I did not make it up, look it up if you don't believe me.'

'Maybe you looked it up in the library already and what you said about your great-grandmother going to school with her was nonsense.' Step was trying to push Alice's buttons.

'I'll have you know that Violet Alexandra Pennyford was very much a student here. If you don't believe me I suggest that you consult the Academy records,' Alice huffed.

'We all believe you Alice, Stef's just messing with you,' Charlotte said.

'I find it fascinating, she was a bird for all those years probably thinking that she'd never be human again. Imagine soaring through the skies,' Gerty held her arms out either side of her and pretended to fly around the room.

'Don't you know any wing spells?' Alice asked.

'I tried one once but it didn't go so well,' Gerty stopped pretending to fly and walked back over to her bed.

'Why, what happened?'

'Well, I ended up temporarily turning myself into a penguin.'

'They're a flightless bird,' Stef laughed.

'I know but I did make a very cute penguin. My mom was certainly surprised when she found me waddling around the kitchen trying to open a tin of sardines with my beak,' Gerty chuckled.

'Penguins are my favorite, when I was younger my parents

used to take me to the zoo and I would scream if they tried to move me away from the penguins. In the end, they took it in turns to stand with me whilst the other one went off and looked at the other animals,' Charlotte said.

'Charlotte making a scene, who'd have imagined that,' Stef smirked.

'Like I said, I really liked penguins,' she grinned.

'I like penguins too but I'd rather be human. Anyway, I'm going to wash this slime off because I stink,' Gerty held her towel under her arm and headed towards the bathroom.

'That's probably for the best, you do smell pretty bad,' Stef waved her hand in front of her nose before she burst into laughter.

'You don't smell so great either,' Gerty laughed back, before she disappeared into the bathroom.

'Do you know a spell to make the weekend hurry up, I want to see what surprise Miss Moffat has for us?' Charlotte said.

'Nope,' Stef shook her head.'We'll just have to wait it out.'

'You girls are so impatient, it's only a few days away,' Alice said, as she tugged her brush through her hair.

Charlotte and Stef both exchanged knowing looks and tried not to laugh.

'I still can't believe that we won, it's the best feeling ever,' Charlotte smiled, as she fell back onto her bed.

'We're a strong team and we have Gerty for a climber so we

were sure to win,' Stef replied.

'Do you think we will face Witchery College again sometime soon?'

'Probably.'

'I hear that it's in a black castle surrounded by a moat of boiling tar, so you better hope that you don't fall off your broomstick when flying over to it,' Alice said.

'Yeah right, I suppose you know that because your great-great-great-aunt was a student?' Stef goaded.

'I come from a very respected wizarding family and none of us have attended Witchery College.' Alice put her nose into the air, how dare any of these lower-class witches make fun of her family.

As the two girls carried on bickering Charlotte closed her eyes and relived the game in her head and a contented smile spread across her face.

Chapter Seven

It was the girls' first lesson with Miss Zara, their fortune-telling teacher and they were all excitedly apprehensive about it.

'I hear that she's strict and that she once turned a second year into a slug for a whole week,' Gerty said, as she walked alongside Charlotte up the hallway.

'Do we have to go to this class, my mother says that fortune-telling is nonsense anyway and that we are in charge of our own fate,' Alice groaned.

'Don't let Miss Zara hear you say that,' Stef said and a worried look appeared on Alice's face.

'She can't be that bad,' Charlotte said, as she pulled on Gerty's arm. 'Come on, let's make sure that we aren't late.'

'And that we get good seats,' Stef added.

They hurried into class and over to the front row, which was the only place where there were four seats together. Miss Zara was sitting behind an intricately carved oak desk, a large glass ball on a stand in front of her. Her long dark hair fell in ringlets down her blue trimmed black dress and she wore a beaded black choker around her neck. She wasn't looking at the girls, instead she was glancing down at the worn-covered book that was in front of her.

The girls exchanged looks between themselves and sat in silence. They didn't dare speak just in case Miss Zara turned out to be as terrifying as she was made out to be.

'I am Miss Zara, fortune telling is what I shall teach you. Unimportant is what you might think this lesson is. You take your spells and your potions, you say they are more useful. I vant you all to understand that my lessons count,' she said in a strong Russian accent.

'Come, come,' she gestured for the girls to gather around her. 'This crystal ball is important, very much so. 'Fortune telling is not alvays correct, because your actions can change your future. However, your futures are all in the crystal ball for this point in time.'

'So you can see what will happen to us in the future?' Demi asked.

'Yes, it is in there. Who will volunteer?'

'Me,' Stef shot her arm into the air.

'Miss, you should choose me to go first, after all I know my future is assured as I do come from a first class witching family,' Alice chimed in and Stef rolled her eyes.

'Yes, Alice Smithers, let's look at your future first,' Miss Zara gave a slight smile as she leaned over the crystal ball.

'The Magic Mirror Company is where you work.'

'Don't you mean I own it?' replied Alice.

'You work the assembly line, installing magical powers into the mirrors.'

'What do you mean by that?' Alice said angrily.

'You know, magic mirror on the wall, I give you the powers to install, yada, yada, yada,' she waved out her hand. 'Don't believe me, see for yourself.'

Alice looked down at the crystal ball and saw a woman with the same mousey brown hair and freckles. It was an older version of herself. She was wearing a long white lab coat with a badge saying 'Magic Mirror Spell Installer,' pinned onto it.

'No, it can't be,' Alice muttered, before she walked back to her seat and sat down in shocked silence.

'Stephanie, your turn,' Miss Zara said. She looked back into the crystal ball. 'Big things vill happen to you Stephanie Jolly.'

'Are they good or bad big things?' Stef asked.

'You are destined to marry the most influential and wealthy wizard in the world. Together you vill rule over a kingdom of magical people and creatures and bring good deeds to your land.'

'Gosh!' Stef exclaimed, her legs beginning to wobble so she leaned against the desk to steady herself.

'Who is he?' Gerty asked.

'You have met him recently.'

'Do you think it's the boy you were dancing with at the dance?' Gerty said.

'I doubt it, he didn't look like he would ever be a powerful wizard,' Destiny said.

'Demi seemed to like him,' Charlotte added.

'I did not,' Demi grunted.

'This is so exciting, make sure you invite us to the wedding,' Gerty clapped her hands.

Stef just stood there speechless before she nodded her head and walked over to her seat, sitting down next to a now even more annoyed looking Alice.

'Gertrude, your turn,' Miss Zara studied the crystal ball. 'Umm, let's see. Ah yes, Gertrude Baggs, you're going to live in the normal world and as a witch you vill be able to help many people around the world. I see you on the world stage as a humanitarian, you are receiving a reward. Let's see, aahh, yes, the Nobel Spell Prize.'

'That's the perfect reading for you Gerty,' Charlotte hugged her friend.

Gerty excitedly jumped on the spot, a huge smile on her face.

'Charlotte Smyth, you are next. Such a big heart you have, full of love and goodness. Charlotte you are going to become a teacher at this Academy. And one day when Miss Moffat retires she shall entrust you to become the principal at this esteemed school.'

The other girls gasped on hearing this and they all looked at Charlotte, who blushed, not knowing what to say.

'Your fellow teachers vill admire your special ability to turn around girls who are on the edge,' she glared over at Demi. 'Into respectful young ladies.'

'That's really great Charlotte, you'll make an amazing teacher,' Gerty wrapped her arms around her dear friend.

'One reading is all I have enough energy left for,' Miss Zara yawned. 'Demi, come closer,' she gestured her forwards. 'It shall be you.'

Demi looked wary as she reluctantly took a step forward.

'Let me see,' Miss Zara fell silent as she concentrated on her crystal ball. 'Demi Taylor, do you like iPhones?' she glanced up at her.

'Erm yes, they're by far the best type of phone.'

'Good, good, because when you leave school you're going to repair shattered iPhone screens in a phone repair factory.'

'What!' Demi shouted.

'It's not all bad Demi,' Miss Zara patted her on the shoulder. 'You are by far the best worker in the entire factory. Every day you will repair hundreds of screens, with a little help from your magic ability.'

Demi stared at her open-mouthed, too startled to show her anger.

'What about my good friend Margaret Montgomery, do you know what her future will be?' Demi enquired, still feeling wounded on hearing about her future.

'Good news, you'll see her every day.'

'Will she be working in the iPhone factory as well?'

'No, but a fast food restaurant is across the road from there, I see her flipping burgers.'

Demi lowered her head, she didn't want to hear anything else Miss Zara had to say about her future as her words were too awful for her to comprehend.

'Remember that the future is always changing, but if you want to change the future...you must change your behavior,' Miss Zara addressed the girls, stopping on Demi.

Demi nodded her head before she looked down at the desk in deep thought.

'Over the coming months I shall teach you how to read the

crystal ball without my help. For today this is the end of the lesson,' Miss Zara gave them all a smile before she went back to reading her book.

The girls all left the classroom, chatting excitedly amongst themselves about Miss Zara's future predictions. They found her fascinating and frightening at the same time and they were all curious to learn how to be able to read fortunes by themselves.

Chapter Eight

The weekend arrived and with it came their reward for winning Save the Princess. The yard had been turned into a party paradise, with a large table full of cupcakes and sweets. There was a constantly flowing fountain, one side of it contained red soda and the other chocolate. There was also a color-changing candy-floss stand. The candy-floss was being spun by large grey owls.

'This is the best party ever,' Gerty said, as she dipped her eighth strawberry into the chocolate side of the fountain.

'It's definitely better than the last party I went too,' Charlotte grinned.

'Look,' Alice pointed up to Miss Firmfeather, who had turned her broomstick into a rhino and was flying above them.

'Girls, who wants a ride?' she smiled down at them.

'Me, me,' Gerty squealed, as she waved her arm in the air.

'Do you think flying is a good idea, the amount of chocolate strawberries you've had?' Alice said.

'I once ate a family bag of chocolate buttons and then went on a plane and I was fine,' Gerty replied.

Miss Firmfeather landed the rhino in front of them and beckoned an excited Gerty forwards. She flicked out her wand at Gerty and made her feet lift off the ground and up onto the back of the rhino. They flew a couple of laps around the yard before Miss Firmfeather helped Gerty down with a spell.

Alice went next and Charlotte and Gerty cheered for her as she and Miss Firmfeather flew around the yard. Stef walked over to the candy-floss stand where a group of second-years were holding a stick of color-changing candy-floss.

'That looks so cool,' Stef said to them.

'You have to get some, the flavors change depending on what color it is,' a girl with waist length blonde hair said.

'The pink is watermelon favor,' a wavy-haired, petite girl said.

'A large candy-floss please,' Stef said to the owl and it held the stick in its beak as it spun it around the candy-floss.

Stef was on her way back over to the others when a giant bubble engulfed her and lifted her up into the air.

'What the fudge,' Stef said, as she she looked down at the ground and saw Sonya and Silvia waving back at her. They blew another huge bubble that surrounded another unsuspecting girl.

'Put me down right now,' the girl shouted.

Stef shrugged before she sat down in the bubble and put her feet up against it, rolling herself forwards as she bit off chunks of her candy-floss.

The other girl in the bubble saw what Stef was doing and copied her, her outcries soon turned into shouts of joy as she rolled around the yard. Soon girls were begging Sonya and Silvia to blow bubbles at them and dozens of girls were rolling around in the huge bubbles.

Stef's bubble lowered itself onto the ground before it popped and Stef walked over to her friends. Charlotte and Gerty both pulled chunks off Stef's currently green candy-floss.

'Yum apple,' Gerty said.

A Beyoncé tune began to blare out across the yard and Miss Dread was using the Save the Princess court for a dance floor.

'Come on girls, come and dance,' she gestured them over.

'I love this song,' Gerty grabbed Charlotte and Alice's arms and pulled them forwards and Charlotte called out to Stef to join them.

Stef stood on the side-line as she finished her candy-floss and watched as the other girls joined in on the dance floor and copied Miss Dread's moves.

'And spin,' Miss Dread said, as she spun on the spot and all the girls copied her.

Stef finished her candy-floss and joined the girls on the dance floor.

Five Beyoncé songs later and the girls walked off the dance floor out-of-breath but in full spirits. They stood on the side-line and retrieved their breath before they walked across the yard.

'Got me looking, got me looking so crazy in love,' Gerty sang.

'What now?' Charlotte asked.

'We haven't been on Dexter yet,' Alice pointed over to the far side of the yard where girls were bouncing on the dragon's belly.

Demi and Destiny were already bouncing on Dexter and Alice eagerly joined them, followed by the others. To start with all the girls were being sensible and careful, avoiding bouncing into each other, but then Charlotte misjudged her bounce and accidentally brushed into Demi's arm. Charlotte thought that Demi would shout at her, but instead she giggled and gave her a gentle shove.

Soon all of them were bouncing high on Dexter, holding hands and laughing.

'Higher!' Destiny yelled, as she pulled on Alice and Stef's hands. 'Let's jump higher!'

Destiny pulled on their hands too much and then they all tumbled down onto Dexter's belly, giggling.

'Do you think we'll get a party like this, every time one of our team wins?' Gerty asked.

'I hope so,' Demi replied.

'It's worth it just for the candy-floss, talking of which,' Stef shuffled her way over to the ladder by the side of Dexter.

The rest of the girls stood back up and grabbed each other's hands before they began to bounce again. Charlotte couldn't hide her smile, she didn't like conflict and she was glad that they were getting on with Demi and Destiny. Winning Save the Princess had shown them that they were a team and they succeeded far more when they worked together.

Alice slowed down her jumping and tugged on Charlotte's arm as she gestured for her to look across the yard. Charlotte stopped on the spot and Demi followed Charlotte's gaze.

When she saw what Charlotte was looking at...Demi abruptly stopped, the smile vanishing from her face.

Standing across from them, her blond hair swiped behind her back and a severe look on her pretty face was Margaret Montgomery. The yard fell silent as the rest of the girls noticed her, including Stef who almost dropped her candy-floss.

Charlotte found herself thinking about the vial of fairy dust that was tucked away in the draw under her bed. She regretted the fact that she didn't have it on her...as she could have done with some guidance right now. The girl who'd nearly got her expelled and who'd turned her into a cockroach, leaving her to be squashed, was back at the Academy.

Margaret looked far from happy as she glanced over at the girls who were on Dexter and who had clearly been having a brilliant time without her. She felt betrayed and angry and she clutched her wand tightly as her gaze remained unfaltered.

Thank you for reading Witch School Book 2!

I hope you enjoyed it!

If you did like Witch School, could you please do me a huge favor and leave a review on Amazon?

Thanks so much for your support!
Katrina x

Witch School - Book 3 : My First True Love

is out NOW!

Here are some more great books you're sure to love!

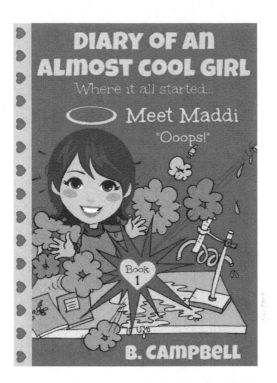

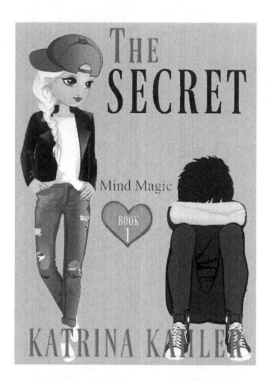

Don't forget to subscribe to our website...

Best Selling Books for Kids
www.bestsellingbooksforkids.com

Then we can let you know when our next book is published.
You can also select a book for free!

Follow us on Instagram
@freebooksforkids
@juliajonesdiary

Printed in Great Britain
by Amazon